UNDER THE HUNTER'S WING

UNDER THE HUNTER'S WING

Peter E. Noon

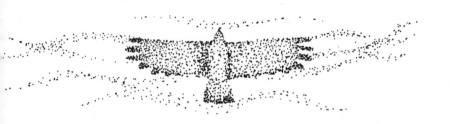

Foreword by
His Grace the Duke of Devonshire,
P.C., M.C.

The Book Guild Ltd.
Sussex, England

The Book Guild Ltd.
25 High Street,
Lewes, Sussex.

First published 1992
Reprinted 1992
© Peter E. Noon 1992
Set in Souvenir Light
Typesetting by Southern Reproductions (Sussex)
East Grinstead, Sussex.
Printed in Great Britain by
Antony Rowe Ltd.
Chippenham, Wiltshire.

A catalogue record for this book
is available from the British Library

ISBN 0 86332 692 7

CONTENTS

FOREWORD
by
His Grace the Duke of Devonshire, P.C., M.C.

Peter Noon's story has particular appeal for me, since it has as its background the Peak District and its hero suffers from severe physical handicap.

It has been my good fortune to be involved with the welfare of the physically handicapped in Derbyshire for many years. I am constantly struck by their indomitable spirit to triumph over their disabilities. This spirit is an inspiration to those of us lucky enough to be sound in limb.

Even for the fittest people, the Peak District is a challenge. The terrain is unique in this country and I, like countless others, find in it a magic quality. Peter Noon, in his book, has brought a part of Derbyshire that I greatly love together with a section of the community for which I have the greatest admiration.

It, therefore, gives me enormous pleasure to write this brief foreword.

The Farmhouse

PART ONE

HERNE'S CHAMPIONS

Herne's Meeting

David sat, staring across the high, bleak moorland to a rocky outcrop, where the land seemed to fall away into the valley below. The houses of the town spreading over the basin of the valley bottom looked very small, like the buildings on a model railway he remembered seeing not long ago on a school trip to York.

A little way back from the dark gritstone edge stood a massive wooden cross. This, according to the guide book his parents had bought in the town the previous day, had been erected by the Church congregations some years before.

David was on holiday with his family, renting a rather primitive old farmhouse on the very edge of the moor, above the spa town of Buxton, in the Derbyshire Peak District. They had arrived quite late the day before after a long drive, and had been forced to ask directions to the farmhouse in a small gift shop in the town. The guide book had come from there.

'Well, I had to buy something,' laughed his father, when he had returned to the car, with a complicated string of instructions which seemed to include rather a lot of 'left turn followed by a right,' and, 'straight out of the town up the hill, by the hospital with the large dome.'

The slow bumpy drive up the mile long track from the main road, in the gathering dark, had seemed very exciting to David and his sister Sara. The first proper look from the windows that morning, had done nothing to dispel the feeling that they were in a different world.

Instead of the neat rows of orderly gardens and parked cars, which was the view David was used to, from the

11

windows of their home in the city, the sun streamed down on bright heather, green patches of rough scrubby grass and the greyish white backs of the sheep. These seemed to be the only other occupants of a landscape wider, and wilder, than David had ever imagined possible.

He was on his own at the window of the small sitting room in the farmhouse. His binoculars hung on a cord round his neck, and a pile of books, about the birds he might see from the window, covered his knees.

The last words of his father, as the others left to buy provisions in the town below them, kept coming back to him.

'You will be all right, won't you?' he had asked. 'We won't be long, and I'm sure you will find something to amuse you.'

'Do stop worrying, Dad,' laughed David. 'I could be happy all day with a view like this to look at, and it says in my book of moorland birds that the sparrowhawk often hunts across the heather, looking for mice and shrews. Wouldn't it be great if I could see one this morning?'

David knew a lot about amusing himself, ever since he had been knocked down by a car outside his home when he was four years old, he had spent his life in a wheelchair. He was twelve years old now, and his life wasn't so bad most of the time. His family and teachers did all they could to make his life as busy, and as full, as possible and David responded well.

He had developed interests and hobbies which he could do from his chair, rather than moping about the sports he was missing. He had recently become quite interested in archery, which he could do at a local sports centre that had good access and facilities for disabled people to use. He had also become a keen watcher of nature.

The birds in his garden at home, and a squirrel who regularly visited his mother's bird table, were a constant source of pleasure to him, as he sat quietly behind a half drawn curtain in the living room watching. His mother or sister would sometimes go with him to the park, which was not too far from the house.

There, he found all manner of wildlife to observe. Although, he supposed, the pigeons and mallard ducks

12

which clustered around the visitors in the park, waiting to be fed on scraps of bread, could not really be wild. They lived their lives amongst the neat, ordered flower beds and properly trimmed lawns, totally dependent on man to provide them with food.

David also spent a lot of his time reading. Books about nature, wild animals and birds filled the bookcases in his room. He had written several articles on wildlife for his school magazine, which his English teacher had praised quite highly.

However, in the quiet times, when his mother thought he was dozing or watching the television, he sometimes couldn't help thinking to himself, 'Why me?'

He tried very hard not to ask the question out loud, as he knew it upset his family to see him unhappy. At those times, he felt bitter and frustrated at the constraints his wheelchair put upon him, and very, very angry at a world which seemed to give so much more to his schoolfriends and his sister, than it did to him.

The sun, and the gentle breeze that blew over the moor, seemed to beckon to him, and he felt that the rather dark little room was growing stuffy and airless. He spun his chair away from the window and rolled through to the much larger kitchen. There, the stable door stood open to the yard, and the moor beyond. He wheeled his chair to the very edge of the doorstep. Locking the brakes with a snap of the twin levers under his hands, he settled back with a sigh.

This was better, he could smell the heavy, honey smell of the heather, and the strange, oily, acid smell of the sheep. He could hear their bleating as they grazed the short grass. Flying insects filled the air with a low droning noise, which seemed to come from everywhere at once, but seemed to stop when he listened particularly for it.

If he closed his eyes very tightly, he could imagine himself running over the moor to the cross, and on beyond the rocks to - where?

'I must remember to ask Dad for a look at the map, when he comes back,' David thought drowsily, as his head drooped slowly forward onto his chest, and he drifted off to sleep, warmed by the sun and lulled by the peace of the scene before him.

It seemed only a moment before he was jerked rudely, and suddenly awake. He tried to gather his scattered thoughts.

'I couldn't have been asleep long,' he thought, 'but I wonder what it was that woke me up. I was sure I heard someone call out. A name? Perhaps my name?'

He looked around, but everything seemed to be as he remembered it. The lane, at least for the last part of its length, where it ran free of the trees on the lower hillside, was empty. The small, stonewalled paddock, where his father would need to park the car, was untenanted.

A strange, shimmering curtain of light seemed to hang for a moment on the edge of the trees, but just as David was thinking that it must be caused by the bright morning sun, it vanished, and the events of the next few minutes carried away the memory, as if it had never been.

He was alone. But how could he be? He was quite sure now, that he had heard a call, and as his eyes swept slowly over the moor in front of him, he became aware simultaneously of three very odd things.

The huge cross on the edge of the moor was no longer there. The valley below seemed to be empty of human habitation. Standing perfectly still, just beyond the farm gate leading to the moor, was a being, the like of which David had never seen in his young life. He was very tall.

'Well over seven feet,' David thought, 'if you measure from the tip of his antlers.'

For antlers he most certainly had. Wonderful, majestic antlers that seemed right somehow, and not at all out of place above the stern, craggy face, browned by the weather, like pictures David had seen of seafaring men who spent their lives on the decks of sailing ships and just as human, he was surprised to see.

The 'man', if man it was, was dressed in a tunic of rough sacking-like material, with leggings of the same homespun, tucked into his soft leather boots. It didn't occur to David to be frightened, or even wonder why he wasn't. It just was not possible that this visitor could mean him harm. He was quite sure of that.

'Have you come for me?' he called, thinking at the same time, 'What a strange thing to say.'

14

'I have,' said the man. 'I am Herne the Hunter, and today we must travel for a short while together. Come.'

'Perhaps he doesn't realize I'm disabled,' thought David. 'We won't be able to cross the moor with my chair.'

He was wondering how to explain all this to his new friend, when he found himself rising to his feet and walking forward by Herne's side. They moved away from the farm and his chair, and with every step the memory of these things grew fainter.

'Come Robin,' cried Herne. 'Your men will have need of meat this night, and it is a fair step to the archer's wall, where the King's deer graze today.'

'Excuse me, sir,' replied David. 'But my name is David, and I think you must be mistaking me for someone else.'

'Nay lad, I'm not mistaken,' laughed Herne. 'We've left David's world a long way behind, or should I say in front, whichever. You are in my world now, and in the world of Herne the Hunter, your name is Robin.'

With every step, Herne's words seemed more real, and the frustrations of his life in a wheelchair became more dreamlike. He was not in the least surprised to discover that he was dressed in a dark green tunic and leggings, or that his feet were encased in tall leather boots like the ones that his companion wore. Rubbing his chin, he discovered that the odd sensation that he was feeling, was caused by a luxuriant growth of beard. The weight of a quiver of arrows and an unstrung yew-wood bow felt good slung across his shoulder.

A shout of pure joy rent the air.

'Robin it shall be then!' he cried, and throwing back his head he began to run out over the moor. He skirted the edge of the valley, where he could see woodsmoke rising from two villages about a mile apart, both built on rising ground, though both still a long way below the high edge upon which he ran. A deep dale ran between them like a sword slash across the countryside.

Somewhere in that wild headlong rush he found himself alone. Herne was not needed now, but Robin was sure he would appear again when the need was presented. He knew who he was, where he was going, and why.

15

Robin at the Archer's Wall

Robin lay very still in the heather, his long bow by his side, and very slowly inched his way around, and behind, the rough drystone wall that marked the edge of the treeline, above the combe and the vale of Chapel en le Frith. As he rose to his knees, to bring his eyes level with the top of the wall, and his quarry back into his line of sight, a rough voice spoke almost at his elbow.

'Well, good sir. I think there will be venison enough for both of us. Do you not agree? There must be three hundred or more grazing in the trees down there.'

Robin dropped again behind the wall, and when he was sure he was out of sight of the grazing deer, he turned to face the speaker.

'I would be interested to know who makes so free with the King's deer,' he whispered.

'People hereabouts call me Brian the Bearward. I live in the village under the Buck Stone yonder. And whom do I have the honour of addressing, sir? I haven't seen you in these parts before.'

'I am Robin, known by the hood I wear. My men and I live and hunt in Sherwood Forest, close to Nottingham. And now, good Brian, to business. Who shall shoot first?'

'Why Robin Hood, of course. Your prowess with the long bow goes before you.'

'Nay Brian, my bow is unstrung, and you were here at the archer's wall before I. So, you shoot first and shoot well. I will take my chance with the second.'

Brian rose to a crouch, pulling the string of his long bow to his ear, and loosing a shaft a full three feet in length, with deadly accuracy at the proud buck, which stood, head thrown back and many pointed antlers outlined against the sky. The buck leapt into the air and crumpled to the ground, shot through the heart.

Robin thumped Brian the Bearward on the back, 'Well shot, sir! Well shot!' he cried. 'You are a man of the forest and I can use men who can shoot as you do.'

Robin then picked his target and drew his bow, again the arrow sped true, and another deer fell dead.

'There is venison pie for my hungry men and I,' he said. 'I would be honoured if you would join us for the feast, Brian.'

Brian did not answer. He was looking down at the edge of the trees. As Robin turned to see what he was looking at, six men ran from the trees, from the direction of Fairfield village and quickly surrounded them. They were dressed in the green uniforms of the forest rangers, and wore on their sleeves a silver shield bearing the sign of a lion rampant, the coat of arms of the King of England.

'Well met,' cried the leader of the foresters. 'What are you two rogues doing here, at the archer's wall. Up to no good, and hunting the King's deer, I'll be bound.'

'Neither this forest, nor its deer, belong to King Richard the Lionheart any more,' replied Robin, 'but to Prince John of Lackland and, by my reckoning, to me, when I and my Merrie Men are in need of meat.'

'Only a traitor, and an outlaw, would talk like that,' roared the forester, and rushing at Robin, dealt him a blow which, if it had landed, would have knocked him unconscious. Robin danced back, expecting the blow. He caught the staff on his bow, and in one fluid movement, raised the hunting horn from his belt, to blow a long, deep, penetrating note.

The forest seemed to hold its breath. The deer in the trees froze, in that split second before explosive flight. Even the birds, whose song was a constant background to the life of the forest, were still and quiet.

The moment of shock was broken by the loud clapping of wings, as a flock of woodpigeon burst from the treetops below the embattled men on the hilltop. As if from nowhere, between the trees appeared five men.

The foresters shifted from foot to foot uneasily. These

17

were odds which were not in their favour. The newcomers were obviously men well used to the long bows they carried in their hands, each with an arrow nocked in readiness. Broadswords hung at each belt. These were Robin's men, loyal to him, and to King Richard, united in their hatred of Prince John, who considered himself King of England in his brother's absence.

First to arrive at Robin's side was Little John. He was a giant of a man, who had been with Robin from his first days as an outlaw in Sherwood, and whose gentle strength had always been a mainstay of the band.

Next came Will Scarlett and Alan a'Dale. Will was a young man of noble birth who had, like Robin, been outlawed when his family's lands were given over to a Norman crony of Prince John's, for some trifling service rendered.

Alan a'Dale was the minstrel of the group. Over the opposite shoulder to his deerhide quiver of arrows, he carried a lute. Many were the times that the information he gathered from the local people in the taverns in which he sang, allowed the band to intercept Prince John's tax collectors on a quiet path through the forest, and to relieve them of the illgotten gains of their profession.

William of Hazelbadge leapt lightly over the wall to stand at his leader's side. He had newly joined the outlaws, as they passed through the parish of Hope, on their way from Sherwood to Peveril Castle. A disagreement with the master of Hazelbadge Hall, over the ownership of a hare or two, had caused him to leave his home and family hurriedly and join the band.

The arrival of the last of Robin Hood's men was preceded by a great deal of gasping and groaning.

'Why must we hunt in a country with so many hills?' he moaned.'Life in the monastery was never like this.'

This was Friar Tuck, forced to become an outlaw himself after being discovered by the Abbot stealing food from the monastery larder, for the outlaws of Sherwood in the depths of a particularly hard winter, some years before. He was very fat, and adopted a whining tone of voice when things were not going his way, but many an adversary had discovered to their cost that, like many overweight men, he was surprisingly light on his feet and a deadly exponent of the art of quarterstaff fighting.

He was dressed in a rough brown robe, as befitted his calling, and was the only one of the merrie men who was not clad in the Lincoln green doublet and hose favoured by the outlaw band. His staff was a blur of movement around his head, as he tumbled over the wall, and the merry gleam in his eye told a very different story from his complaining grumbles of a few moments before.

'Hold back, lads,' laughed Robin. 'The forester here seems to think he and I have a quarrel to settle. I would like you to see fair play.'

'We'll do that gladly, Robin,' said Little John, moving swiftly to the side of the largest forester, and putting an arm round his shoulder in a friendly fashion. 'Much better that our two leaders sort this out, than all of us fighting. Is it not, my friend?'

The forester took careful note of the strength in the arm on his shoulder, and the size of the hand resting, as if by accident, on the hilt of his sheathed short sword, and agreed with alacrity.

'That's right, friend. 'Tis only a deer after all, and Prince John cannot eat them all, now can he?' he replied with a very nervous chuckle.

The eleven men formed a loose circle on the hillside. Robin passed his bow and quiver to Friar Tuck saying, 'Mind these for me Tuck, and do me the honour of the loan of your sturdy quarterstaff.' So saying, he turned towards the centre of the circle with a smile on his face and the staff held in the guard position across his chest.

Robin and Ralph, the forest keeper, began to circle warily around each other, within the circle. For several moments neither attempted to strike a blow. The moment when a missed strike runs out of power is an extremely vulnerable one, and neither man wanted to risk testing an unknown adversary.

Robin led with a series of feints, but Ralph was not to be drawn from his defensive stance. He was sure this man was an expert, and his slow, methodical countryman's mind was fitting together pieces of a puzzle, which had been bothering him.

'Who is this man?'

19

He was sure that he knew everybody who lived in his village of Fairfield, and the neighbouring village down in the valley, called Buck Stone after the very spot on which they now fought. He was sure that this man was not from either village. He spoke like a gentleman, and his bearing bore out that upbringing. Yet he wore the Lincoln green of a forest outlaw, and was the leader of a band of men, who were prepared to defy the laws of the land, with a casual disdain.

Ralph feinted to Robin's side. Robin dropped his staff to block the bow. Reversing his grip on the staff, Ralph struck Robin a full blooded blow on the side of his head. Robin staggered back several paces, shaking his head to clear his wavering vision. He tried desperately to defend his abused shoulders, around which Ralph's staff was beating a tattoo.

As the pain cleared from his head, Robin began to realize that Ralph had made a vital mistake. He was sure that his opponent was confused and disorientated, and that it was only a matter of time before he won the contest. Robin let his staff slip loosely through his hands, giving Ralph the impression of a defeated man. Ralph took the bait; stepping back he raised his staff for the final blow.

That blow never found its mark. Robin stepped swiftly forwards, and brought down his staff with a resounding crack, on the forester's head. Ralph fell to the ground, stunned.

Robin turned, and called to Brian the Bearward, 'Bring your buck Brian, and if William will fetch mine we will be on our way. I think we have earned the right to a good supper tonight. My invitation to you still stands, come and sup with me and my merrie men.'

Ralph's men gathered round their stunned leader. Most were trying, not too successfully, to hide their smiles. It was not every day that the forest keeper met his match, and the story would be worth several flagons of ale in the tavern in Fairfield that night.

Robin and his men were a hundred yards away across the hillside when the answer to his puzzle came to the befuddled forester. He had been hearing rumours in the village for several days, that Robin Hood the outlaw, had been sighted in the Peak Forest. The story had it, that his love – the Maid Marion – was travelling with the Prince in the north of the county, and had been staying at Peveril Castle for some time, whilst Prince John hunted the Royal Forest.

This must be he. His men had called him Robin, and was it not well known that the notorious outlaw was of gentle birth. Ralph leapt to his feet, a deer from the King's herds would never be missed, and he had been fairly bested, but to allow Robin Hood to escape, when every soldier who travelled with the Prince was out in the forest searching for him, was another matter.

Taking up his long bow, he took careful aim at Robin's retreating back, and let fly an arrow. Robin and his friends were laughing as they crossed the hillside, recounting the details of the fight to each other, to be sure that Alan a'Dale would be able to put the action to song, when the time was right. Ralph's arrow struck without warning, knocking Robin to the ground with a groan of pain, and making his men grab for their weapons whilst searching the barren hillside for cover. A flight of arrows soon discouraged the forester's men from any further attack, and they set off at a run to the village, to raise the people to help hunt down Robin Hood.

Little John fell to his knees beside Robin, and examined his wound. The arrow had entered his back, just below the shoulderblade, and had luckily become embedded in the heavy muscle there, rather than passing through to pierce a lung. Friar Tuck quickly took a small knife from his belt, and carefully cutting the arrow through about an inch above the skin, roughly bound the wound with a strip of cloth from his pack

'That will stop the bleeding until we can get him to a place of safety,' he said. 'But if we wait too long to remove the arrowhead, then I do not know what will happen.'

'There was a troop of soldiers at the King's Head Tavern in Peak Forest village when I passed through this morning,' said Brian. 'It will not take the foresters long to get a message to them. If your men are camped in the forest near Peveril, then we would be running into their hands to try to get Robin back there. I know of a place where we can hide, in the valley below the Buck Stone. 'Tis a cave, which is used by one of our local outlaws, and is not known to the soldiers.'

Little John stooped and carefully lifted Robin in his arms. 'We must be on our way to this cave then. Robin is badly hurt, and we are exposed on this hillside for all to see.'

Escape to Poole's Cave

The outlaw band wound its way down the hill, leaving the combe and the view over Chapel en le Frith behind them. Skirting the village of Fairfield on the hillside to their left, they found themselves confronted by two natural barriers. Immediately in front of them ran a swift flowing river. Brian the Bearward called it the River Wye. It meandered across the valley floor, at the foot of a limestone bluff, which was perhaps seventy feet in height. On the top of this craggy, flat-topped hump of rock, was the village of Buck Stone. Several insubstantial paths wound their way down to the river from the houses above.

Brian led the men to a place where large rocks had been dropped in the water, to make stepping stones. They all made the crossing safely, although Little John did not find it easy with Robin in his arms. On the further bank Friar Tuck stopped, and looked up at the rim of the cliff above him.

'Must we always be climbing up, or falling down, this wretched countryside?' he groaned. 'What wonders have the people of Buck Stone to hide that they build their village in such an inaccessible spot!'

Brian laughed merrily.

'When you have lived in the Peak Forest for a while, you grow accustomed to the hills, good Friar. But do not fear! We have no need to climb the cliff to reach the village. Our path takes us behind the grove of trees, and round the bottom of the rock to the hiding place I told you of.'

The party of fugitives moved hurriedly into the shade of the edge of the trees. Walking quickly across the short springy turf, they left the shadow of the cliff behind them, and began to climb the gentle slope of the opposite edge of the valley.

They were soon standing under a huge overhang of limestone, partly screened by bushes and scrub. When they were all inside, safely hidden from prying eyes, Brian told them to wait for him, disappearing towards the back of the cave.

'Where is he going?' whispered William of Hazelbadge. 'There can be nothing back there. 'Tis solid rock.'

'Hush William,' said Friar Tuck. 'He seems to be a good man to have on our side. Robin appears to trust him, and that is good enough for me. So we will wait here, as he told us to, but be alert and watch the mouth of the cave.'

No sooner had the ex-monk finished talking, than Brian's face appeared high up in the rocks at the back of the cave.

'Bring Robin up here,' he called, and the others started with surprise. When they had scrambled up the rock, they found that a small passage led away back into the hillside. It soon opened out as they followed it into a dark damp cavern.

Small sounds echoed, and the sound of running water seemed to come from everywhere at once. There was a feeling of being in a large open space. When Brian stirred the embers of a fire, which was smouldering in a large side chamber, the flames leapt towards a high domed ceiling, and it became obvious that they were in a cavern of truly great proportions.

Standing by the fire was a great bear of a man. His clothes were in rags, and long, filthy hair reached to his shoulders.

'This,' said Brian, indicating the unkempt figure, 'is Poole. I'm afraid he doesn't do so well from his trade as the outlaws of Sherwood. However, he chooses to live here in this cave, and scratch a living by relieving the travellers who pass through here from Cheshire, of their purses. Many rich merchants come this way to the Great North Road.'

'We thank you for your help and hospitality,' murmured Robin weakly. 'We are in need of a place to hide while my wound heals, and this would seem to be well hidden.'

'You cannot stay here for long,' replied Poole. 'The cold

and damp in this cave never changes, no matter what the weather outside, and it is not the place for a man to heal. I do know of another hideout that would suit you better, but it is some miles away. You cannot travel any further now. Stay here tonight, and I will show you the way in the morning.'

Friar Tuck skinned and dressed the bucks, which Brian the Bearward and William of Hazelbadge had carried throughout all their adventures slung across their broad shoulders. When the meat was clean, he rubbed it with herbs and crushed rock salt from his pack, and set the two deer roasting over the fire on a large iron spit, which Poole kept for the purpose.

The great fire burned cleanly, using as it did elm and beechwood which had been gathered weeks before by the outlaw Poole and stacked to dry slowly just inside the great overhang of rock which protected the cave's entrance from the elements. What little smoke there was rose straight to the high domed ceiling of the cavern and escaped, undetected through the thousands of tiny fissures in the limestone to the wooded hillside above.

Soon the cave was filled with the delicious aroma of cooking venison, and all the men gathered round hungrily. The company feasted upon a hearty meal, although Robin ate very little, and was in obvious pain from his wound.

When the meal was done, Brian took Little John a few steps into the cavern to speak to him.

'I must leave you now for a while,' he said softly. 'I am sure that those foresters we met, at the Buck Stone today, will have recognized me. I have no doubt that they will report my presence with your party. I must away to my home in the village, to warn my parents and say my farewells. It seems likely I will be joining Robin Hood's Merrie Men for a while.'

Little John placed his huge arm around Brian's shoulders and embraced him roughly.

'I hope all will be well with your family, Brian,' he said. 'We would not have faired so well today without your help. We will be honoured to have you join us.'

Brian gathered up his bow and arrows and slipped out into the night, making for the track into the village.

It was not far to his house on top of the bluff, and from his angle of approach from Poole's cave, not too steep a climb. He crept quietly between the huts of his neighbours until he reached the wattle and daub dwelling which he shared with his father and mother. Pulling aside the curtain of sheepskins which hung over the doorway, he slipped inside. It was apparent immediately that news of his troubles had preceded him.

His father paced the room, which occupied all of the interior of the hut, making no effort to avoid the several dogs which scurried from his path, at every circuit of the central fire pit. His mother sat, quietly mending his leather overjerkin as he had seen her sitting hundreds of times before. This evening, however, as she sewed, she cried softly to herself. Her tears fell unnoticed onto her work.

Brian did his best to appear cheerful.

'Now Mother!' he cried. 'Nothing can be as bad as that. I must go away for a while, that's all. I could not ask for better companions. When the soldiers leave the forest with their master, Prince John, I will be able to return and lead my life as if nothing had happened.'

'You may well be right, my son,' replied his father, 'but do not tarry here too long this night. The soldiers have been here already seeking you, and they will be back again in the morning.'

Brian kissed his mother. Wishing his father a fond farewell, he began to gather up his few belongings into a bundle. Soon he was on his way back to Poole's hideout, and his new friends. His father watched as he left the village, his heart heavy. When would he see his son again, he wondered?

☆ ☆ ☆

When Brian left the fireside in the cave to visit his family, Robin's men arranged themselves round the fire. Poole smacked his lips and wiped the grease from his beard.

'It's an ill wind, they say, that blows nobody any good,' he laughed. 'And that was some of the best venison I've tasted for many a while. If the hue and cry for Robin Hood has passed us by in the morning, then the springs below the village would be a good place to visit. That arrow must be dug out soon, and people around these parts do say that the water from these springs has the power to heal.

Now, tell me how the famous outlaw, Robin Hood, and his men come to be hunting on the hills around the Buck Stone. I'd have thought there would be richer pickings in Sherwood.'

'Richer pickings, indeed,' laughed Alan a'Dale. 'Life needs more than money, however, to make it worthwhile, and our leader is in love with a maid.'

'I should have known!' growled Poole. 'I've heard it said that Robin Hood would do anything for a pretty face, or a good fight. I can see now that it's true.'

'Nay,' returned Alan. 'That is not the way of it at all. Settle round the fire and listen. I will tell you the tale of Robin and Marion, and of how we came to be here.'

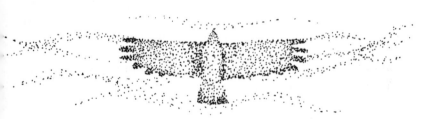

Alan's Tale

'The maid I mentioned,' began Alan, 'is the Maid Marion, the fairest maid our city of Nottingham has seen for many a year. With long fair hair, and the softest brown eyes you have ever seen, she turns the heads and hearts of every man she meets. And yet, is so good natured that none, not even the ladies of the castle, hold that against her.

'She lives in Nottingham Castle, in a small apartment, with her mother and their maid. Her father fell from grace in Norman eyes for some trifling offence, and had to flee the county.

'She has taken the eye of Sir Guy of Gisburn, a hard and evil man. He is almost as hard as the master he serves, Prince John of Lackland, who has made him keeper of Nottingham Castle and chief tax collector for the whole of the County.

'Sir Guy has decided that Marion shall be his bride, and has been trying to persuade her for many a year, to say yes to his offer of betrothal. Marion will have nothing to do with the man, and is only barely civil in his presence. She cannot, however, let her feelings show, or things will go hard for her mother, who is a virtual prisoner in the castle. It is very difficult for Marion to keep her true affections locked in her heart. You see, she is already deeply in love with an outlaw.'

Alan let his glance slide to the fireside, where Robin was sleeping uneasily, the pain from his wound causing him some discomfort.

'Marion met, and fell in love with, Robin of Loxley when they were both children, playing children's games in the castle grounds, and through the streets of the city of Nottingham,' he said softly.

'Robin's father, the Earl of Loxley, spoke out for the rights of his fellow Saxons too strongly, and too often. He died defending his family, and his manor, from attack by Norman soldiers, sent to arrest him, and drag him in chains to the dungeons below Nottingham Castle.

'Robin escaped unnoticed, a youth in the homespun clothing of a forest lad, and took up residence in Sherwood. He was clothed and fed by the common folk of the many villages deep in the greenwood, but his will to live survived only by a deep, all abiding hatred of all things Norman.

'He put his skill with long bow and sword, learned at his father's knee and from the Master of Arms at Loxley Manor, to good use. He would waylay Sir Guy's tax collectors and the occasional rich Norman bishop as they travelled through Sherwood Forest. The taxes they had collected from the common folk of the greenwood, he would return to their rightful owners.

'Gradually, as word of this young champion of the people spread through the forest, men came to find, and to join him. Some were like himself, honourable men, with a wish to see England free from the crushing taxes imposed by Prince John.

'Some were petty thieves and vagabonds, with very few scruples and large families to feed. But mostly, they were just men, ordinary men, fallen foul of the Norman lords, and needing to hide in the forest until they could venture home again. From all this dissident crew, Robin has forged a band of fighters second to none in the land, fighters with courage, fighters with skill, and most of all, fighters with hope.

'Throughout all their years in the forest, Marion's love for our young outlaw has grown. She visits our camp whenever she can slip away from the castle at Nottingham. She has become part of the lives of all the men in our band. She attends to their wounds after skirmishes with the soldiers. She eases the homesickness of the men, who cannot visit their families for fear of capture, by delivering messages to and from our wives and families, on her rides through the forest.

'Any one of us would gladly give his life for the Maid

29

Marion. So it seemed a small thing for the band to travel north, following Prince John, who, I am sure you have heard, is quartered at Peveril Castle in the parish of Hope on the edge of the Peak Forest.

'He has taken advantage of the particularly dry spring and good travelling conditions, to visit the northern regions of his brother's land. Gathering the taxes, "for King Richard's Holy Crusade," so he says, and to hunt the royal forests as he goes.

'He came by way of Nottingham and the forest of Sherwood to Peveril Castle, which as I am sure you know,' said Alan, 'was the home of the Earl of Peveril, keeper of the King's forest and protector of the peace within it.

'It is so no longer; the earl lies now, in his own dark dungeon. Prince John has the idea that he was involved in the poisoning of the Earl of Chester some little time ago. He has confiscated the castle, therefore, and all Peveril's lands and possessions, "in the name of the King" of course. He has put some lackey of his own in charge of the castle and the forest.

'He is even now enjoying the hunting with his Norman friends, for John of Lackland does not visit alone. His whole court travels with him, and since his visit to Nottingham, Sir Guy of Gisburn dances attendance upon him.

'Sir Guy, of course, insisted that Maid Marion should join the royal party, no doubt hoping for a chance to impress her with his closeness to the prince. He should know Marion better. She cares for no Norman, and it is common knowledge that no one is close to Prince John. He has servants, and he has enemies, but he has very few friends.'

When Alan's story came to an end, he stretched out his long legs to the fire, and sat back with a yawn, whilst John took up the story.

'That is our tale, Master Poole. We look to the safety of our own Maid Marion, and a journey such as this one holds no terrors for us. We have no home but the forest, and venison tastes much the same wherever you are,' chuckled the deep voice of Little John. 'The small fact that wherever the prince goes, his tax collectors follow close behind, has only a small bearing on our journey. Now, 'tis long past time we went to sleep.'

So saying, he stretched out on the rocky ground and began to snore loudly.

'How he thinks we may sleep through all that noise,' grumbled Tuck, 'is beyond me.'

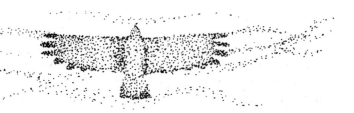

Healing Waters

The sun was hot the next morning as the men gathered round the rough stone table, to which Poole had led them, and on which Little John had laid their leader. They had made their way across the grassy meadows to a grove of trees, which grew over a large part of the valley bottom and shielded the path of the small but strongly flowing river.

This was the River Wye that they had crossed the night before. According to Poole it had its start in the very cavern in which they had spent the night.

The outlaws had skirted the grove the previous evening, having had no reason to enter the trees. So it was with great surprise that they now saw that the wood was threaded with many small streams, which seemed to spring out of the ground and flow quite rapidly, to add their water to that of the Wye.

'Now here is a strange place,' whispered Will Scarlett. 'There is a feeling of peace and kindliness here, which I can feel deep in my bones.'

The other men nodded, and murmured to themselves, relaxing in the shade of the trees. Little John sat down by the side of one of the springs and let his hand dip below the surface, intending to take a drink of the crystal clear water.

He jerked his hand back with a surprised exclamation, 'Why bless my soul, Will!' he cried. 'This water is quite hot. How can that be?'

Brian the Bearward laughed delightedly, 'That took you by surprise, Little John, I'll be bound.' He chuckled. 'These hot springs have risen here for as long as anyone can

The Grove of the Goddess

33

remember. The Romans, who came here hundreds of years ago, called it the Grove of the Goddess, and believed that her power of healing was in the water. That belief still holds strong today with some of the folk hereabouts, as Poole told you last night.

In fact this bench that Robin is lying on, is part of a building which the Roman people built over the springs, long since fallen into decay and vanished. The stone was used to build the hearths in the houses of Fairfield and Buck Stone, no doubt.'

Robin was suffering from a fever, rambling meaninglessly about his childhood in Loxley, and his days in Sherwood with Maid Marion. He did not seem to feel the pain when Friar Tuck began to probe the wound with his knife.

Soon the Friar was able to pronounce the wound free of foreign matter. Will Scarlett brought the warm, healing water from the springs to bathe the freely bleeding wound. The party spent the rest of that day camped around the springs, hiding when the villagers from the hill came to the river for water, and resting up for the journey they knew lay ahead.

From time to time, small troops of soldiers, wearing the livery of Prince John, could be seen riding the hillsides and the high edge which stretched away to the west towards Cheshire, and the plain which ran down to the Welsh mountains.

Towards evening, Poole appeared again, and led them to a track which left the village and ran to the west, over the lowering edge and on to the small market town of Leek.

'This is the route that you should follow,' Poole told them. 'If you make to the north on the top of the ridge, you will drop down into a deep valley, on the edge of the manor of Swithamley. You must then cross the river Dane. The way is marked from there, if you know what to look for. Others of my calling have had need of a place to hide in the past, and so I have hidden signs that ordinary men would not find remarkable.'

Robin was feeling better. His fever had abated, and he seemed once again his old self, although very pale and weak. After another night spent in the safety of Poole's cave, they set out to find their way to the hiding place.

The track was steep, and once again the weather was hot and sunny. What had seemed a boon the day before, when everyone had been resting beneath the trees, now became a curse. As the day wore on and the sun rose in the sky, the outlaws climbed ever higher.

Several times they were forced to seek shelter in the long grass, gorse and wild bilberry, which grew in profusion by the side of the path, as the keen eyed men of the forest sighted mounted soldiers and rangers on foot, searching for the outlaws in the distance.

Soon they were out on the open moor. Cover and shade became hard to find. The shrieking cries of the flocks of curlew, that lifted into the air as they passed, threatened to alert the whole moor to their presence. Luckily for them, however, the search parties were drifting further to the east, concentrating their efforts away towards the Peak Forest, from where they knew Robin and his men had come.

Robin began to weary, and as he swayed, his feet began to stumble over the rough track. John once again picked him up and strode forward, seemingly uncaring of the weight of his friend.

At last they dropped steeply down into the valley of which Poole had spoken. Crossing the wide, shallow river, which flowed through it, they began to climb again through the trees. They followed the tiny signs left by Poole to guide his friends to the hidden chasm in the hillside.

This would be their home until Robin was well enough to travel, and the Prince's men, who were searching the land around Fairfield and Buck Stone, for the most wanted man in England, had returned to Peveril Castle and their master.

The deep scar was narrow, and ran for many hundreds of feet back into the hill. Tall trees grew about its perimeter and it was possible to walk quite near to the edge without knowing that it existed.

Some of the outlaws gathered wood from the ground under the tall trees to make a fire. Others brought in bundles of fern leaves and bracken to make a comfortable bed for their leader.

Robin tossed and turned for four whole days and nights, feverish from the festering wound below his shoulder. He would sleep uneasily for many hours, only to wake up feeling more tired and ill than when he went to sleep.

As he slept, he dreamt strange disturbing dreams. He could never quite remember these dreams when he awoke, but misty pictures of a small, pale boy, dressed in strange clothing and sitting in a small, wheeled cart of some kind, lingered behind his eyes as consciousness returned.

On the morning of the fifth day after their escape from Buck Stone, Robin woke feeling much better, his fever had broken during the night and he could feel strength flowing back into his body with every passing movement. Friar Tuck was bending over the cooking fire, attending to a crude wooden spit upon which were roasting several rabbits.

'I could use some of the meat, good Friar,' called Robin softly. 'I feel as though I haven't eaten for a week!'

Tuck spun on his heel to stare delightedly at his friend. 'Robin!' he cried. 'You are back with us again, in the land of the living. Praise heaven for your recovery.'

He passed Robin a smoking rabbit, wrapped in several layers of dock leaves to shield his fingers from the heat.

'Now you must eat and build up your strength so that we may be on our way back to the forest. John has been watching the road to Leek and has talked with several travellers who have passed through the Peak Forest. The search has been abandoned and the soldiers have returned to Peveril in readiness for Prince John's ride to London. His visit is over, and soon he will make for Nottingham and from there, on to London, before the autumn weather sets in.'

After supper had been eaten that evening, Robin declared himself well enough to travel in the morning, and Friar Tuck called the men about him to hold a small service of thanksgiving for Robin's safe recovery. As their prayers filled the rocky cleft, Robin lay back and let his eyes travel over the edge of the rock above him. He felt a strange reluctance to leave this place.

Somehow, he was sure, his fate was still tied here, and the thought of leaving in the morning seemed very remote and unimportant. It was almost as if it was to happen to someone else, and not to him.

As his gaze once again swept the shadows of the lip of the defile, he thought he saw a strange, dim, dancing curtain of light spread across the small segment of lighter sky above him. He blinked his eyes several times, and when he looked again, it was gone.

Robin looked back at the men, standing or sitting on the ground in a group around Friar Tuck, by the fire. They were softly singing a hymn now. The ancient words seemed to take on more meaning in this sombre setting, and Robin raised his eyes to the sky again as he allowed his voice to blend in with the others.

He started in surprise. Then he looked closely at the base of the trees growing near to the edge above him. Standing in the shadows was Herne, looking down on the scene below and in particular, it seemed to Robin, at him.

A voice spoke in his head. It was very obvious that nobody else could hear, but Robin heard quite clearly.

'It is time for us to travel on,' said Herne.

As he spoke, the hymn swelled to much greater proportions, and the beautiful clear tones of a woman's voice soared above all the others, as the singing climaxed in one ringing heartfelt Amen.

Ludchurch

Henry and the Lollards

Robin felt a flutter of panic as the scene changed before his eyes, but over all the strangeness was laid an aura of calm, emanating, no doubt, from the   presence of Herne the Hunter, the ancient god of this land, who still held sway over his subjects.

The sombre, slow thinking spirits of the trees, the knarled old oaks, the tall dark majestic pines and larches which had grown, cast their seeds and died here, rotting back into the rich peaty ground to feed their saplings in the natural cycle of creation.

The lighter, laughing elements of the short lived plants, the fern, the bracken and the mountain ash, which grew in great profusion from every crack and crevice in the millstone grit of the walls, and the myriad tiny flashes of life and simple consciousness that were all the birds, small animals and insects that lived in the forest. All of these were Herne's subjects, and the passage of time, and the affairs of town and city, meant nothing to them nor to him.

There had been a time, in the distant past of the world, when Herne had cared for the doings of men, but men had begun to change, to draw away from nature and the way of life that Herne knew and had control over.

Only rarely now did he find a member of the race of men to take an interest in, and then only with a certain kind of man. He had to be the sort of man who lived close to the land, but with intellect enough and the insight to take time to look, and to wonder at the marvels about him every day of his life.

In every age there are just a few such men. Robin Hood

was one, and in a later age Henry Montain was another.

The service in Ludchurch, the deep cleft in the hill, in which, the legend ran, the fabled Robin Hood had sheltered and worshipped with his men, over two hundred years before, was coming to an end. Henry shivered as he shook off the strange feeling of kinship, which he felt for a fleeting moment as he thought of the famous outlaw.

Henry was the chief forester, set to watch over all the forest of Leek for his master, the Earl of Chester. As he watched the people take their leave to return to their homes, in the scattered farms across the moor and in the wooded valleys below them, he was troubled and unhappy by the events that had made him what he was, a traitor to his lord, and to his king!

And yet, how could it be that a man who loved his country with all his heart and soul could, even if only in his own mind, be branded as a traitor.

'It's a cruel world we live in,' thought Henry, 'when a man can be persecuted because he thinks differently to another.'

Henry Montain was a Lollard, a follower of the religious teachings of a man called John Wycliffe. The King, Henry the fourth of England, had declared such teachings unlawful, as they called for radical change in the way that religious services were conducted, and that church funds were administered.

The way that had been considered proper for centuries, placed enormous power in the hands of the clergy, and John Wycliffe felt strongly that the church should be more open in its dealings with the common people. English should be used instead of Latin and the bible should be easily obtainable and readable by everyone.

Henry believed with all his heart that these teachings held the seeds of a new way forwards for the people of England. He was sure that they would help the people themselves shape their destiny, and have some choice in the way they lived.

There were almost sixty families living in the valley of the River Dane, which spread out from the hill into which Ludchurch ran. Most of them followed the teachings of Wycliffe, and in their hearts were Lollards through and through.

Most of his fellow Lollards in the Leek Forest lived normal lives, as Henry did, going about their day to day business, working on farms or in the forest to make a living. Some were weavers, candlemakers or cobblers, supplying the population of the forest and the towns around it.

Leek, Macclesfield and Buckstone all held markets and fairs in the summer months, where a tradesman could sell his wares and buy the necessities of life for himself and his family. It was only in their hearts that the Lollards felt different from their neighbours, and here in Ludchurch, that difference could be allowed to surface and to be expressed in song, as they gathered to worship in their own style.

This way of life was denied to some, however. The Lollard preacher and leader in the forest was Walter De Lud Auk, from whom this natural cathedral in the forest had taken its name. He was a hunted man.

He had spoken out bravely to the leaders of the church, in defence of Wycliffe and his teachings, and had refused to recant his beliefs, when ordered to do so by the Bishop of Chester. This, in these troubled, cruel times, was enough to see him driven from his home and hunted like an outlaw by the King's soldiers.

He had crept to the door of the house of Henry Montain some time before. The soldiers were hot on his heels and a March wind had brought sleet and hard driven snow to scour the hillsides, making travelling all but impossible. Henry had brought the elderly preacher in, wrapping him in warm rugs and giving him hot milk with honey and a small dose of French brandy added to warm him and to restore his flagging strength.

Just a few moments after Henry had seen Sir Walter safely installed in a small hidden room behind the fireplace, the rattling drum of hooves sounded on the cobbles of the yard outside and the rough accented voices of the soldiers came to him through the heavy oak door.

'He'll not be here at the house, sir,' one of the voices had cried out. 'This is the home of Henry Montain, the chief forester.'

'I know,' had come the reply. 'Spread out over the hill and report to me here if anything is seen of him. We'll run the old

41

priest to ground tonight, I'll be bound!'

For several hours after that, Henry had been forced to entertain the officer of the troop of men, Captain Jonathon Miller, who had seen an opportunity to combine his duty with a modicum of comfort, to supper and the warmth of his hearth. Sir Walter had crouched hidden, not ten feet away, terrified throughout the long meal that he would make some slight noise and bring disaster upon himself and his host.

The Captain was not a hard man, just a soldier obeying his orders and doing his duty as he had been taught to see it. He had been detailed to bring this errant Sir Walter De Lud Auk to justice before the court in London, and that was what he intended to do.

As the dawn broke over the edge of the moor, and flooded the wooded hillside and valley bottom with a bleak wintery light, Mistress Mellor, Henry's ageing housekeeper, had come to gather the clay mugs and wooden salvers which were all that was left of the supper she had laid out for her employer and his guest before retiring the night before.

The cold, wet, dejected soldiers began to report to Captain Miller in the yard, handing the reins of their horses over to Hal Mellor, Mistress Mellor's husband and ostler cum stableman in Henry's household.

'Not a sign anywhere Captain,' shivered the Sergeant of Arms. 'I'll wager a month's money that old man has spent a warmer night than we have. He'll be hidden somewhere in the forest, in the home of one of his followers, and the men have had enough of this weather and wild country for a good bit.'

In the stables behind the house, the men had been fed a hot meat broth and newly baked bread from Henry's kitchen. They had ridden away still grumbling about their bad luck, and in lower voices, about how their Captain seemed to make his own luck whilst leaving them to theirs.

Sir Walter had remained hidden in Henry's house in the valley until late April, when the weather was warmer and travel more possible. This relaxing of the grip of winter, however, brought with it problems for Sir Walter and Henry, which soon became pressing.

Word of the preacher's escape from the soldiers, and how

this had been achieved, soon filtered through the forest and the surrounding moor to all the members of Sir Walter's congregation.

The path to Henry's door was soon quite busy with Lollard followers coming to seek spiritual guidance, his blessing for marriage plans, and baptism for the babies of the valley.

This situation could not go on. It could only be a matter of time, until these unusual comings and goings were noticed and reported to Captain Miller. He had taken up quarters for himself and his men at an inn, the Pig and Whistle, in the market square in Leek, whilst he continued to search the woods, hills and high bleak moorland between Leek and Buckstone.

Henry spent many hours in deep conversation with Sir Walter.

'You must go away,' Henry said, 'away from the district altogether, until things change for the Lollards as surely they must one day.'

But Sir Walter would not hear of it. 'I cannot leave my people in the forest,' he said. 'You have seen how they have need of me to help them keep their faith strong, and I believe that this is my role in life in God's eyes.'

Nothing would stir him from this view, and so it was decided that he must move from the house to a place of concealment, on the hillside where his followers could come and go through the woods without remark. There, Henry could keep him supplied with food through the summer months.

Several days before Sir Walter was due to make his way, under cover of darkness, to the cleft in the hill which was to become known as Ludchurch, Henry and Sir Walter received a visit which filled them both with joy. Alice, Sir Walter's niece, had made the journey from his old home to be near him in hiding, and the prospect of sharing this time with Alice delighted him. She was a devoted follower of the Lollard way, and had always helped him in his services when they had been held in his home.

Henry's source of joy at Alice's visit was slightly different. He had always been a confirmed bachelor, living his busy life without feeling the need of a female companion, but when his eyes fell on the slight form of Alice De Lud Auk, and he saw her obvious concern for her uncle, his heart was lost.

He had not believed that such a beautiful form could hold a spirit that was as gentle as it was good and kind. He knew that in the days to come, he would do his best to make her his wife.

Henry had instructed Mistress Mellor to make up a bed in the small room in the attic of his home for Alice. She had been grateful for his kindness.

There was little space under the massive beams which supported the thatch of the roof, and she was sure that in the winter months many cold draughts would whistle through the narrow space. But it was spring now, and the little room seemed cosy and bright with the sunlight, which filtered through the small open slits in the wood and plaster work of the gable ends of the building.

When Alice had hung her few belongings from a row of wooden pegs, driven into one of the beams for just this purpose, she washed off the dust and dirt of travel in the oak slatted bucket of water that Mistress Mellor had provided from the well at the edge of the woods behind the house. She changed from her heavy riding habit to a lighter high-waisted kirtle in a fine brown woollen material, and made her way back to the large room at the front of the house where her uncle and Henry were waiting.

As Alice reached the door to the room, through which she could hear the muffled sound of male voices, she paused nervously, her hand raised to knock.

'What is the matter with me?' she thought crossly. 'I have no reason to be afraid.' But the hand that was raised continued on to smooth down her long fair hair, and a sparkle appeared in her soft brown eyes, in spite of herself.

This tall, good looking young forester, in whose house she found herself a guest, had impressed Alice far more than she cared to admit.

She knocked gently on the door, pushed it open and entered. Henry turned quickly from his conversation with Sir Walter, and crossed the room in long strides to take her hand, and kiss it in greeting.

He smiled warmly. 'We were just discussing the coming May Day fair, which is to be held in Leek in two days time, and to which I must go. I need to sell a newly weaned colt from my stable, and to buy several items for the household and my work, which I cannot buy in the Dane Valley.'

'I would consider it an honour, Mistress Alice, if, with Sir Walter's blessing of course, you would accompany me. It is always a boisterous affair, and I am sure you would find it interesting.'

Alice smiled, and looked across to where her uncle sat by the fireside.

'I would love to go, if my uncle does not mind,' she said.

'Of course not my dear,' replied Sir Walter. 'I know you will be safe with Henry, and will have an enjoyable time. You have been much away from the company of people your own age for a long time now, and it will do you no harm to indulge yourself, instead of me, just this once.'

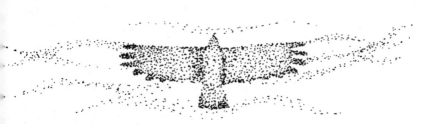

The Leek Fair

Dawn was still an hour away when Henry and Alice met in the cobbled yard in front of the house the following Saturday morning. It was the first of May and the day of the fair.

Hal held the bridles of Henry's large dark hunter, and the smaller dappled grey, which was the horse Alice had ridden from her home on her visit to her uncle. His other hand held a leading rein which was passed around the neck of a skittish young colt, not long weaned from its mother and seeming to be all long legs and nervous energy.

Henry and Alice had not taken time to eat, as they intended to make an early start to the day. The decent horses and all the good buyers would be gone by ten o'clock. Henry did not want his spirited little colt sold to someone who would ill treat him. Nor did he want to have to bargain for his price with the rough horse traders, who travelled from fair to fair in the summer, buying cheap and selling for a small profit at the next gathering.

After they had been riding for a little time, Henry pulled a parcel wrapped in white linen from his saddle bag and, opening it, passed over to Alice a cold roasted pigeon and some crisp new bread.

'Mistress Mellor would not hear of us leaving without breaking our fast,' he laughed. 'She seems to have packed us enough food to last all day. I have some cheese and cold boiled bacon in here for when the pigeon is gone, and an apple tart or two for dessert!'

As the horses picked their way out of the Dane Valley, the two travellers ate and talked and laughed like old friends, and it seemed only a short time until they were riding under the massive gritstone edge of The Roaches, a jumble of broken toothed rocks which appeared very threatening to the tiny figures on the road below.

Soon they were riding into the market place in Leek, which had been transformed from its usual busy appearance, with the people of the town coming and going about their business, into a complete bedlam of seething, shouting humanity.

Stalls had been set up around the edges of the square from which every manner of wares were being sold. Pots and pans were both being offered for sale and old ones brought for repair.

Vegetables from the fertile Cheshire plain below the hills were on sale. Honey and honey cakes filled the air with a sickly sweet smell, which set the crowds of children, who darted under foot, to gathering in hungry groups near the stalls.

Several traders were offering leather goods. Tack for the horses, boots for the men and dainty shoes for the ladies and children, were laid out in rows with cured rabbit skin, for trimming cloaks or lining winter riding coats, displayed between them.

Through all the milling crowd of townspeople, farmers, tradesmen and travelling folk, threaded hawkers with heavy trays balanced on their heads or slung around their necks on a leather strap.

Almost anything you wanted to buy could be bought from these vendors, a hot mutton pie, a bag of herbs or a cure for an ache or a pain. Some also sold love potions, 'guaranteed' to make the wench of your fancy look fondly upon you, or the most eligible bachelor in the town come knocking on your door.

In the middle of the square, the important business of the day was being conducted. Farmers stood with the leading reins of the horses they wished to sell in their hands, or strolled from horse to horse, trying quite successfully to look completely uninterested in the best examples of breeding, as they weighed up the horse, and the man who was selling it. It was just as important to these careful hill farmers to go home with a good bargain as it was to go home with a good horse.

Here and there in the milling crowd, a small island of stationary spectators would build up around a juggler, or a fire-eater, or perhaps just two village lads fighting for the right to take the same pretty young girl to the bonfire and the dancing. These would be held on the edge of the town when the fair was over and darkness had fallen.

Henry headed directly through the crowd to the Pig and Whistle, and took the horses through the archway into the stable yard. Helping Alice from the saddle, he called to the ostler to rub down and feed the horses sparingly, as they must be in good condition for the ride home later that evening. Then, turning again to Alice, he smiled.

'I shall be about my business for an hour or two,' he said. 'Do you think you can find amusement for yourself until I have finished?'

Alice laughed gaily, 'What makes you think I do not have business of my own, good sir?' she cried. 'I have ribbon to buy, some leather gloves and a good warm cloak for Sir Walter. He will have need of it shortly, I'll be bound. Go about your business, Henry. We will meet here in two hours time, our business done and the rest of the day to enjoy the fair.'

'Just a word of warning then,' Henry's face had turned stern and serious now. 'These fairs can be dangerous places, so do be careful, and watch what coins are given to you by traders. There has been a lot of Flash money passed at these fairs in recent years, and as you know, it is utterly worthless.'

'It is sweet of you to worry,' replied Alice, 'but I will be very careful. I have seen Flash money before, so I will know what to look out for.'

Henry took the rein of his colt and led him out into the melee, intent on finding a good spot from which to display the horse, and Alice set about her shopping with a will.

She soon had the ribbon she needed, and a little bit extra. This was of an unusual shade of green, which she really couldn't resist. The gloves were next on her list, and soon a very attractive pair of soft brown leather were hers for not much more than she had intended to pay.

The cloak for her uncle proved much more difficult. There were two stalls selling the sort of heavy woollen material and the rabbit skins which she needed to make up the cloak, and Alice was thoroughly enjoying the indecision she felt.

She was torn between a very smart, but light weight dark brown cloak and a tan cloth of altogether heavier weave, which would be warmer for Sir Walter, but never make him look as distinguished as the dark.

As she crossed the market square between the two stalls that held her attention, she became aware of a disturbance near a booth selling pots and jugs of ale, which was much frequented by the rougher element of the crowd. She stopped at the edge of the cheering, jeering mob, and peeped through them to see what was happening.

At the centre of the disturbance was a soldier in the King's uniform. He appeared to be complaining to his officer that the ale seller would not serve him, although it seemed from his appearance that this had not been true for very long.

The confrontation bore all the marks of developing into a fight. Alice turned, to slip away before the trouble could spread. Already several of the soldier's comrades were making their way to the scene, with the uncanny instinct for a fight that is characteristic of their kind.

As she turned. Alice was relieved to see the tall figure of Henry, pushing his way through the press towards her.

'What is going on here?' he asked as he reached her side, putting his arm around her shoulder to shield her from the worst of the pushing and pulling that was building up in the crowd, as the people at the back tried to find a position from which they could see.

'I am not sure,' replied Alice. 'There would seem to be some kind of disagreement with the stall holder.'

Henry stiffened with surprise as he looked over the heads of the people in front, and suddenly began to push his way forward towards the ale stall, rather than backwards to where Alice considered safety lay.

She had no other option than to move forward with Henry to the front of the mob. From there he called, 'Good day, Captain, is there anything I can do to help?' In a low whispering aside, he said to Alice, 'Do not contradict me whatever I say, and follow my lead in all things. I will explain later what is happening.'

Alice could only nod her head in silent agreement.

Captain Miller turned towards the sound of Henry's voice. With a look of relief on his face, he explained the situation.

'This rogue will not serve my man here a jug of ale, as he maintains the fellow's money is no good, which is patently a nonsense as I gave it to him myself this very morning.'

'And may I ask how you came by it, Captain?' smiled Henry.

'Why sir, I changed several gold pieces from my pay chest with the money changer over yonder, in order to pay the men before the fair began.'

Captain Miller threw out his arm to point at what was very obviously one of the few empty pitches in the busy market place, and stood with his arm half raised in some confusion.

'I assure you, Sir, the man was there not a half hour ago,' he spluttered. 'I cannot think where he has got to.'

'I can,' said Henry. 'I suggest you pay the ale seller from your pocket, round up your men, take back the money you gave them, and meet me in the Pig and Whistle as soon as you can. I can explain what has happened here very easily, but as you and your men are strangers, I could not expect you to understand without a lengthy explanation. This is not the place for that just now. This crowd could turn ugly at any moment.'

After fifteen minutes had passed, the Captain entered the main room of the inn and looked around. Seeing Henry seated with Alice at a corner table waiting for him, he crossed the room and bowed curtly.

'Well, Master Montain,' he said, 'I hope you can indeed clear this up for me. My man tells me that the seller of ale kept on saying that he could not take his coin as it was Flash money. But that, however, made no sense to him, nor to me.'

'It does to me,' smiled Henry, 'but first allow me to present to you my cousin, Alice. She has travelled from her family's home near Lincoln to visit me for a month or so, and I naturally asked her to accompany me to the fair.'

'I am enchanted to meet you, Mistress Alice, and I hope your stay here will be a happier one than mine is turning out to be.' Captain Miller bowed over Alice's hand and lightly kissed the back of it.

'Why thank you Captain,' smiled Alice, hiding her confusion by lowering her gaze to the floor in a pantomime of modesty. 'I am enjoying my visit greatly.'

Captain Miller turned back to Henry, 'And now, Sir, if you please, the explanation.'

'High in the hills, above the valley of the Dane, on the road towards Buckstone, lies a hamlet by the name of Flash,' began Henry, 'and in this hamlet, through the long winters that we are prone to here, the travelling people and fair folk set up their winter quarters on a farm called Pastures Farm.

They find this location very suitable to their tastes, as it is so near the border of the two counties. If trouble should approach from the Derbyshire side, in the form of the Sheriff's men, then it is easy to slip over the border into Cheshire and, of course, to do the same in reverse when the need arises.'

Captain Miller shifted impatiently in his seat, 'But what is all this to do with my man and his Flash money? I fail to see where your story is leading us.'

'Have a little patience, my dear Captain,' soothed Henry. 'These hawkers have very little to do in the long winter nights, and so they occupy their time making use of a button press, to make counterfeit coinage, which they then distribute, mixed with real coins at the summer fairs.

Your money changer must have been one of those rogues and, I am afraid, you will have paid your men with at least some of the worthless Flash money.'

'I suppose you are right,' sighed the Captain. 'I must collect the useless coinage from my men who are waiting outside, and repay them in proper coin of the realm. I thank you for your help and explanation, I shall check very closely in the future, before accepting money anywhere in the vicinity of the village of Flash.'

Alice and Henry returned to the fair to enjoy the time left to them before setting out for the valley, and home. On the ride back, Alice asked for an explanation of Henry's story about a cousin from Lincoln.

She was more than satisfied that he had acted correctly, and thought very quickly, to save a potentially dangerous

51

situation, when she learned that the Captain was the same man who hunted her uncle, Sir Walter, so ardently. The woods rang with their laughter as they returned to the valley recounting the story to each other as they went.

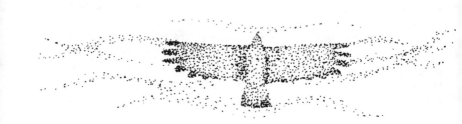

Discovery

As the summer had progressed, the Lollard following had held many services in Ludchurch. Sir Walter had settled into an uneasy peace, living in the cave which Henry had shown him at the far end of the cleft. He rarely ventured out beyond the narrow, rocky entrance to the 'Church'.

Henry and Alice had been regular visitors. At least twice a week they had made the journey up through the pine trees with a sack of provisions for Sir Walter. As Henry's friendship with Alice grew, and their respect for each other became more deeply rooted in familiarity, so too grew their love.

Henry's scattered thoughts returned to the present as Alice shook his arm lightly and asked, smilingly, 'Why so serious, good sir? You appeared to be a long way away from me in your thoughts just then.'

'Away from here only in time, and not away from you at all,' Henry answered. 'I was thinking of how we met, and of how Sir Walter came to Ludchurch.'

Another service was over. The congregation had dispersed to their homes and Henry and Alice returned to the house in the valley. A house which seemed warm and full of life to Henry since Alice had been his guest.

Mistress Mellor had prepared a meal of cold roast mutton, cheese and bread from the larder, ready for their return. As they ate, they talked in the easy informal way of friends who are sure of each other, about the coming months, and the work that must be done to spread the Lollard cause to other parts of the country, and indeed, beyond the English shores to other countries where the clerics held an unjust sway over the common people.

The time passed in routine work until it was time to make the trip once again up the hill, broken only by one incident which left Henry feeling very uneasy. He and Alice were just about to sit down to supper when Henry was drawn to the window by the sound of a horse in the yard, and looking out, he saw that his late visitor was Captain Jonathon Miller.

'How strange,' chuckled Henry to himself. 'It always seems to be a mealtime when the good Captain calls.'

Turning from the window he spoke quickly to Alice, 'I think it would be better if you were to develop a headache, my dear,' he smiled. 'Although, I'm sure one of the reasons Captain Miller is here, is to see if my pretty cousin is still visiting me. I think it would be best if he did not get too much of a chance to question you.'

'I think you may well be right,' replied Alice. 'That man worries me a little. I feel sure that behind his rather bluff, bumbling exterior, lies a clever man. I will go to my room until he leaves. I trust you will make my excuses to your visitor.'

Alice left the room hurriedly and Henry followed. Crossing the hall, he threw open the front door.

'Hal,' he shouted. 'Come and take the Captain's horse to the stable.' Then lowering his voice and extending his hand, he moved out into the yard.

'Good evening, Captain,' he smiled, 'and what brings you such a distance from the Pig and Whistle? Come in and take some supper with me. I was just about to eat.'

'Why, that is very kind of you,' replied the Captain, feigning surprise at the invitation. 'I had no idea it had got so late. I'm riding the forest paths in search of information which could lead me to the Lollard, Sir Walter De Lud Auk, but it seems he has disappeared. No-one seems to have seen hair nor hide of him since that night in March when we tracked him almost to your door.'

There followed what to Henry seemed a very uneasy silence, broken only when Captain Miller asked, 'Are you eating alone, sir? Has your cousin returned then to her home in Lincoln? She will be sorely missed, I'm sure.'

'No,' Henry replied. 'Alice is resting in her room. She was feeling unwell a little earlier, and Mistress Mellor has taken her up a tray.'

54

The conversation drifted to the Lollard beliefs, and seemed to run in the same vein throughout supper. Henry found it difficult to play out his part as a forester with little or no interest in the doings of the Lollards.

However, after what seemed an age, the Captain rose to his feet, gathered his leather riding gloves and helmet from the oak stand in the hall, and took his leave, saying, 'We shall catch the man yet, Henry, have no fear. And, when we do, anyone who can be proved to have helped or hidden him, will make the trip to London, and a dungeon, with him.'

This piece of information, tossed casually over the departing shoulder of the Captain, held all the menace of a direct threat to Henry's guilty mind. He did not worry for himself. He had been a follower of John Wycliffe's for a long time and had always known the danger, but now he had a new worry. The very thought of his Alice being dragged in chains to London, by rough unmannered soldiers, made the blood run cold in his veins.

For several hours, the Lollard congregation had been making their way in ones and twos, and by varying paths, to the narrow rocky entrance to Ludchurch, in order that suspicious eyes should not notice the influx of people to the woods.

Now all were assembled and ready for the service that was about to begin. It had become the habit of Sir Walter to ask Alice to lead the gathering into the singing of the first hymn, as her voice was so good and clear. This occasion was no different from any other.

Henry thrilled as he always did, as the voice of his love rose higher and higher in perfect pitch and harmony, and the assembled worshippers joined in the responses. As the last notes of the song died away into the echoes and the natural cathedral-like stillness returned to the rocky defile, Henry heard the clicking of hooves on stone outside the entrance.

Before he could react, a loud voice boomed out, calling all within to yield themselves up in the names of the King and the Bishop of Chester.

Henry leapt to block the narrow entrance, drawing his sword as he moved forward beyond the rocky portal, to confront Captain Miller and his men who were grouped on the path outside.

'Well! Well!, said the Captain. 'Henry Montain! I was beginning to wonder about you, but I was not sure you were involved. That is why we searched this part of the forest today, and the voice of yon nightingale did the rest. We could not help but follow the sound of her singing. I gather from my enquiries around the countryside hereabouts, that your "cousin" bears a strong resemblance to the niece of your preacher, Sir Walter De Lud Auk. It is strange, is it not, that they should have the same name?'

Henry raised his sword, crying out loudly for all to hear, 'You may have found us at our worship, Captain, but you will have to pass me if you want to take any prisoners this day.'

He was hoping to give as many of the Lollards as he could, time to make their way to the other end of the cleft, and to scramble up the rocky slope on to the moor. One of the soldiers, however, in the closely packed group around the entrance, saw the upward movement of Henry's sword and, believing his captain to be in danger, he quickly drew his pistol, pulled back the hammer bearing the flint, aimed and fired.

The shot was high. The soldier had been afraid of hitting Captain Miller, but as the pistol kicked in his hand, it rose higher still, and as the ball flew from the brass bound barrel, over the shoulder of Henry Montain, it struck Alice De Lud Auk where she stood, surrounded by her friends and fellow worshippers, behind Henry on the rising path through the rock.

Alice screamed as she fell forwards. Henry spun on his heel in time to see his love crumple to the ground. With a roar of rage, he turned again, and began to beat back the soldiers with his sword.

Two of the luckless men fell to his anger before a strangely moving sound began to intrude on the clashing of swords and the cursing of the fighting men. The gentle followers of Sir Walter were gathered around the body of Alice. Not one had thought of escape in their grief, and now, led by Sir

Walter himself, they were singing a dirge for their beautiful young singer.

As the rich, slow cadence of the hymn rolled over the combatants, the fighting stilled. Henry, the Captain and all of the soldiers still on their feet, gathered round, brought together by the tragedy, which no-one had intended to happen.

Captain Miller dropped to his knees beside Alice. He began very gently to examine the terrible wound in her side. Looking up, he singled out Henry where he stood, distraught and hopeless, with his head turned to the rock, tears of remorse coursing down his face.

'I think she lives, Henry,' he whispered. 'She is badly wounded and is losing blood at an alarming rate. However, she is young and healthy, and I do not think that the bullet struck any vital organ as it passed through her side.'

A great joy spread over Henry's face, and from there it progressed to all the people in Ludchurch. Worshippers and soldiers alike fell to their knees and gave thanks in their own way for the deliverance of Alice.

When order had been restored, Captain Miller officially arrested Henry and Sir Walter, which was, after all, his mission. A litter was made of branches and the soldiers' coats, to carry Alice down the hill to the house where Mistress Mellor would be able to care for her.

Alice lay in a coma for three days. The men had placed her gently in Henry's bed, in the large bedroom, which occupied most of the first floor of the house. Mistress Mellor dispatched her husband to Leek to bring back the surgeon healer, who had a practice in the town.

Hal arrived back at the house on a lathered horse, with the healer following closely behind. Henry, who had given his word to the Captain not to try to escape, took him up directly to Alice's bedside.

After a lengthy examination, he stood back from the bed, smiled at the anxiously waiting Henry, and pronounced Alice to be very ill, but in no immediate danger. Captain Miller's earlier assessment of her condition was proving to be the true one.

'With rest and good care,' the healer told the assembled group of men, as they gathered around the fire later that day, 'she should be as well as ever she was in the fullness of time.'

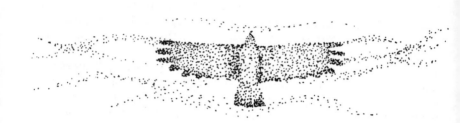

Herne's Parting

For three, seemingly endless, days of waiting, Alice remained unconscious. Henry paced the floors of his home in a frenzy of anxiety, whilst Captain Miller interviewed all the Lollards who had been involved in the service in Ludchurch on the day that she was shot.

At last, Alice opened her eyes and asked, very faintly, for Sir Walter. He arrived hurriedly, puffing and blowing at the bedside. She took his hand and asked how he was, was he being treated well by the soldiers, and was Henry alive and well. Her last memory on the day she had been wounded, was of seeing him standing alone in the entrance to Ludchurch, sword in hand, facing a large party of the King's soldiers being led by Captain Miller.

Her uncle sat down in the chair by the bed, and explained in great detail, the events leading up to the present time. He related how he and Henry were under house arrest, but that Captain Miller seemed to be a fair and just man who appeared to have some sympathy with his prisoners.

'I sometimes feel,' he confided to his niece, 'when we are talking late at night, after the guards have gone to sleep in the stable where they are quartered, that the good Captain could almost agree with the teachings of John Wycliffe, and that he is a little divided in his loyalties.'

The following morning Jonathon Miller called his two prisoners to attend him in the parlour of Henry's home. When Sir Walter was comfortably seated, Jonathon told them of the decisions he had made during his long and sleepless night.

'The Mistress Alice is well on the road to recovery now,' he began, 'and I must tell you what I have decided. I am a professional soldier, and my loyalties lie with the King and the Church, I cannot, and will not, gainsay that. But in all my life as a soldier, I have never faced such an unpleasant duty as is before me now.

'I have seen and talked to all your followers who were present when you were taken. I am satisfied that they are simple folk, who were led into the teachings of Lollardy, without knowing what they were doing.'

'But that is not so!' began Sir Walter angrily. Jonathon interrupted him with a wave of his hand.

'Hear me out, man,' he said softly, and continued as if nothing had been said. 'As I find this to be the case, I have decided to send them back to their homes and their families, albeit with a warning to be seen in church with enormous regularity in the future. What is in their hearts and minds is beyond a simple fighting man such as I.'

'Thank you, John, from the bottom of my heart,' smiled Sir Walter. 'Whatever my fate is to be, I shall accept it with good grace, knowing that my people are safe here in the valley.'

'I can do nothing for you, Sir Walter, save to ensure that your trip to London is a comfortable one,' admitted Jonathon. 'You are the reason for my being here and I cannot go back to London without you.'

'I realize that,' replied Sir Walter, 'but do not worry. I have had a great deal of time to think these last three days, and I feel now that, perhaps my place is in London. We followers of Lollardy have hidden our beliefs for too long. We must confront the clerics and the nobles with our ideas and our ideals. What better platform could I ask for than a public court?

'I shall in all probability fail in my task, but I am growing old, and my course is almost run. That matters not. Our reforms will go on. They will be carried forward by younger, more zealous men than I, until this land becomes a better place for the common people to live in, through the teachings of John Wycliffe and others like him. That is all that really matters in the end.'

Captain Miller was visibly moved by the old priest's obviously sincere statement, 'I am glad for you, Sir,' he said.

'We will make our journey to London a slow one, and as we travel, you can tell me more of this Lollardy of which you feel so strongly.'

He turned to where Henry Montain was standing quietly, looking out of the window at the view across the River Dane and the wooded hillside beyond.

'I think you know your fate, Henry. One of my men will never use his sword arm again, and one I will leave behind here, buried where he fell, beneath that great oak tree at the mouth of Ludchurch. I cannot overlook that.'

Henry nodded slowly, 'It is what I expected, Captain. I must pay the price for my rage. I cannot tell you, or any man what foul blackness came over me when I thought my Alice dead, nor the remorse I have felt in my heart ever since. But no matter. Your man lies dead at my hand and I expect to hang for it when we reach London.

'I thank you for all your kindness to our people, and I too will have reason enough to wish the journey a slow one.'

The Captain smiled, 'I was about to say,' he said, 'before you made such a pretty speech, that if a man were to escape into the forest from this window, I would not have the slightest hope of recapturing him before I had to leave for London.'

He turned on his heel and left the room. Henry followed as he strode towards the great oaken front door of the house. He paused with his hand on the latch. Turning back, he looked directly at Henry and said, 'I will place a guard outside this door for the hour it will take my men to make ready to ride. As you will be secure here inside, I release you now from your promise not to attempt to escape.' He smiled again, sadly. 'Goodbye Henry,' he added in a quieter voice. 'I hope we shall meet again one day, in happier times.' Henry hurried upstairs to say his farewell to Alice. He told her of all that Captain Miller had said and of his hopes for the future. Gathering her gently in his arms, he whispered, 'I will return one day soon, my love. Until then I would be honoured to consider us betrothed.'

'Oh, Henry!' Alice replied. 'Of course I will marry you. No finer man exists in all the world. But where will you go until the hue and cry is forgotten, and you can return to me?'

'I have family in Lincoln, remember?' Henry answered

with a wry smile. 'I will make my way there. Then on to Boston to take a ship carrying wool for France. I hear the Church there can be hard on the common folk.'

☆ ☆ ☆

The sun shone down on Henry as he rode slowly over the moorland track which would lead him to the village of Buckstone, and from there to Lincoln and safety. He was sure that if there was a search being conducted for him at all, then it would be in a completely different direction to the one he was taking.

He thought fondly of Captain Jonathon Miller as he rode, letting the horse pick its own way along the stony path, paying little attention to his surroundings. Suddenly he looked up.

Something strange was happening to the moor ahead. A dancing, sparkling curtain of multicoloured light was sweeping towards him. Henry had never seen anything like it in his life before. He started instinctively to turn his horse away. Before he could complete the turn, the strange phenomenon had swept over and past him.

He noticed as he swung back in the saddle that whatever it was had vanished. It did not continue to rush across the moor behind him, it simply was not there at all. It was as if he had been its focal point and its destination.

Henry looked ahead. Everything seemed the same, except for the figure of a man, who appeared to be waiting for him, just below the rise of a low hill some way in front.

As he drew nearer to the figure, Henry could see that it was Herne the Hunter, a being, that, as far as Henry was concerned, he had not the slightest knowledge of, before passing through the curtain of light.

'Good day to you, Herne,' called Henry, wondering as he spoke if he was really Henry Montain, or Robin Hood, or just David Watson.

Herne seemed to read his thoughts with ease, 'You are all three of them,' he said, 'and many more besides. In every age of the world, I have need of a champion. A man who will protect my subjects and my lands in that age. Come, let us walk together and I will explain a little more as we go.'

David looked vaguely round. Hadn't he been sitting on a horse? Well, no matter. He stepped lightly out by Herne's side and as they walked towards a dilapidated old farm-house, which David could see in the distance, looking rather familiar, Herne began to talk.

'This ancient land has always been my land,' he said, 'from shore to shore, and sea to sea. In the beginning my subjects were all who inhabited it, the animals, the birds, the insects and of course, the people.

'However, as the ages passed, man changed. He was no longer content to take what the earth gave him, and to live in harmony with his fellow creatures. He struggled with me for dominance over the natural balance, which I maintained over the land, and as he poisons more and more with his industries and his greed, so I have retreated to the wilder, quieter places of my kingdom.

'In the seeds of man's greatness, his inquisitiveness, his restlessness, and his constant search for a better way of life, lie also his ultimate downfall. In his eagerness to grow and to change, he disregards all that is old, and tested and true. He destroys anything he cannot control and turn to his own advantage.

'Man will never successfully challenge me and mine, for I know the end of things, as well as the beginning. I know that if at last, greedy man had his way, and my kingdom was no more, then would the world end for all things.

'My champions through the ages must work to prevent this. You have touched, on this journey of ours, the threads of the lives of two such men. They have fought the wrongs and the evils they have found in their own time, and they have helped to keep the wild places free for all my subjects. Do you understand now why we have travelled together?'

'I'm not sure I do,' muttered David. 'I am disabled. Without your presence I cannot walk, let alone fight. What good can I be as your champion?'

Herne smiled. 'No age of the world is the same as any other, David,' he said softly. 'The evil men and the wrong doers take different forms in each, and so my champion must develop new weapons with which to fight them.

'Your age is the age of the pen, not the sword, and this must be your weapon. You have always had a deep love for all my subjects. That is why I chose you. In your future you will be known as a writer of great works. You will draw the attention of the people to the importance of my world. It will not matter to them that you cannot walk. Do not let it matter to you. You have the opportunity to do more than all my champions of the past, to save our worlds from destruction.' Herne's voice softened, 'I must leave you now, for a while at least. Remember my words and my trust. We will meet again when I have need of you.'

The sound of a car, working hard to climb the lane from the main road, woke David from a deep sleep. He was sitting in the doorway of the farmhouse in his wheelchair, the warm sun bright on his face. He waved to his family as they climbed out of the car loaded down with shopping.

David felt strangely confused, as though he had been having a vivid dream and was now struggling to understand what was reality and what was the dream.

His sister Sara ran towards him waving a sheaf of leaflets. 'There's all sorts of things to do here,' she called. 'We've been to the Tourist Information Centre in the Crescent and we've picked up all these brochures. Did you know Buxton is a spa town, and that it was first developed by the Romans?'

'Yes,' smiled David. 'I did,' and taking the leaflets from his sister, he asked, 'Did you find anything about a place called Ludchurch in the Dane Valley. It's not far from here, and it's very pretty.'

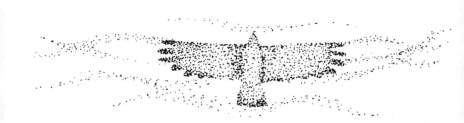

PART TWO

THE HIDDEN VALLEY

Return To The Peaks

The hum of the powerful engine seemed to echo the tune that was running through David's head. He had just passed a large sign for Derby. He knew from his map that the next exit from the motorway was the one which would take him to the road towards Ashbourne, and from there along the high moorland way, which seemed to be crossing the roof of the world to his destination.

He was heading for the Peak District spa of Buxton, and the specially modified van seemed as eager to reach the graciously old world town as he was.

Adrenalin, driven by excitement, coursed through his veins in a way he could not remember ever feeling before. He was still elated with the memory of his graduation ceremony the day before, and he was looking forward to revisiting the high market town where, he felt, had begun the course of his life which had led to the university in the first place. He had been working and studying for a degree in English for three long, hard years but he was sure now that all the work and the uncomfortable hours at his desk had not been misspent. He would never have thought it possible, in his childhood years, that his parents could be so proud of him. His younger sister, Sara, had watched him collect his diploma from the principal of his college with eyes that shone with pride.

Sara had a particular reason for the pride in her brother. Ever since the hit and run driver had knocked her brother down outside their home in the quiet suburban street in London, she had felt a closeness and a responsibility for his wellbeing that many ordinary families could never feel. She had spent hours pushing his chair round the local park, or crouching, often wet and miserable, beside him on a variety of uncomfortable mud flats and marshes whilst he gazed, completely captivated, at the birds and wildlife around him.

Sometimes, just very occasionally, she had felt that her parents were neglecting her a little, whilst they did their best to help David over a particularly difficult patch of growing up with his disability. She knew in her heart that it wasn't really fair or even particularly true, and she dismissed such thoughts quickly when they popped, unbidden, into her head. On his graduation day, however, she had been quite sure that all the little things she had almost unconsciously given up had been worth it.

David smiled to himself as he negotiated the slip road and the great traffic island, which served to slow the cars and heavy lorries from the motorway.

'I really have been very lucky,' he thought. 'I have the prospect of a good career in front of me, doing the only thing I have ever wanted to do, studying and writing about nature. I wonder if things would have been the same if Mum and Dad hadn't brought me to the Peak District when I was twelve years old for that holiday?'

It was on the first sun drenched morning of that holiday that he had been visited by the supernatural spirit of this wild and untamed land, a being with the horns of a magnificent buck deer and the face and body of a man. He was Herne the Hunter, and he had ruled over the wild places of the British Isles, and the animals that inhabited them, for untold centuries. David's life had been changed by that meeting. He had thought constantly, as he had grown towards manhood, of the task that Herne had given him then. It had shaped his thinking and nurtured his ambitions to become a writer and naturalist.

Now, as David drove towards those same towering peaks and dark mysterious dales, he wondered if he would meet Herne again. Indeed, he wondered if it hadn't all been the dream of a small boy, who longed to fight and run and play with his friends instead of living life from the sidelines in a wheelchair.

Perhaps returning to these wild hills would be a mistake,

but whenever reality threatened to engulf him, he found himself remembering Herne's last words as they parted all those years ago.

'Your age is the age of the pen, not the sword, and this must be your weapon,' he had said. 'You have always had a deep love for all my subjects. That is why I have chosen you for my Champion. In your future you will be known as a writer of great works. It will not matter to other people that you cannot walk. Do not let it matter to you. You have the opportunity to do more than all my champions of the past, to save our worlds from destruction.'

Herne's words had proved true for David, he had already established himself as a writer of some repute. The four wheel drive van he was driving was the realization of a dream he had been harbouring throughout all his time at university. He had saved the payments he received from many thousands of words written and published on his chosen subject for a variety of wildlife magazines and radio programmes. As graduation had drawn near he had ordered the van, and when it was delivered, had had it given over to the university engineering department for some of his friends to work on.

They had started by removing all the interior trim, seating and controls and rebuilding them to fit David's particular disability. All the controls were now operated by hand and instead of a driving seat there was an empty space with grooves on the floor, into which David could lock the wheels of his chair. The section of flooring immediately behind the wide back doors was cut away to make room for a hydraulic lift. This could drop to ground level when the doors were opened and lift the wheelchair up level with the rest of the van floor, allowing David to roll forward into the driving position. Just behind the replaced passenger seat was a small, caravan style kitchen, with a calor gas cooker, tiny refrigerator and small sink. Water was stored in a tank under the floor of the van and fed to the tap by an electric pump, On the opposite wall was a foldaway bunk which had been situated at the right height for David to transfer to his wheelchair easily, in case he needed to spend a night in position during one of his wildlife 'safaris'.

By every window was an arrangement of angled brackets

which would hold a camera and binoculars. Lockers lined every available stretch of wall, and cupboards above the kitchen unit held plates, cups and cooking utensils in specially designed racks. He really did feel more independent in this 'hide on wheels' than he had ever done before. It felt extremely good.

He was sure that with this go anywhere, off road vehicle, he would be able to seek out some of the rarer species of wildlife in the less accessible parts of the Peak District. As the smoothly spinning wheels of the van carried him ever nearer to his destination, the feeling that he was returning not only to the Peaks, but to Herne grew constantly stronger.

By late afternoon David was passing through Ashbourne. Setting the nose of his vehicle pointing upwards to the deep blue sky, he changed to a lower gear and began the long climb out of the town, up into the hills which surround and protect Buxton from the encircling industrial cities. Mile after mile of grey drystone wall rolled by, connecting the small moorland farms with a spiderweb of limestone threads. Here and there a coppice of tall trees, beech, elm and sycamore, broke up the smooth passage of the almost ever present wind which roared or whispered, according to its mood, over the mountain pastures.

It was while he was passing one of these small tidy woods that he became aware of a shadow flickering across the windscreen of the van, and appearing to flash on and off as the light from the westering sun shone through the trees. He glanced upwards through the smoked glass of the large sun roof over his head and eased back the hand throttle to slow the van to a crawl.

Floating over his head was the menacing, predatory shape of what he took to be a hawk. Judging by its size it must be quite low, he thought, and yet, something seemed wrong to his experienced eye. He pulled half off the road, stopped, reached over and flicked the switch which would roll back the glass panel, whilst groping on the seat beside him for the ever present camera.

As the sunroof rolled out of sight, David raised the camera. The bird flicked one lazy wingtip and slid rapidly and effortlessly out of sight behind the trees. David lowered his camera with a groan and sat for a moment rerunning what he had seen through his head.

'How very odd!' he thought. 'If I didn't know it was impossible, I would swear that was much, much bigger than the usual sparrowhawk one sees hunting up here. I could almost believe it was an eagle!'

Goyt Valley Encounter

The rest of the journey passed uneventfully, and it was not long before David was dropping down out of the hills into Buxton. He had booked for his holiday into a hotel in the town which he had seen advertised in his daily newspaper. It promised facilities for disabled travellers, and the manager had assured David over the telephone that he would have no difficulties with his wheelchair. Nevertheless, he could not help a small amount of doubt. Lots of well meaning hoteliers and publicans are of the opinion that their premises are accessible to wheelchairs, simply because they do not understand the problems and restrictions which life in a wheelchair must impose on the user. The manager of this hotel, however, had seemed to understand quite well.

'I can always sleep in the van for a night,' he thought to himself.

His fears seemed to be groundless on this occasion though. He found the hotel without any difficulty, and was relieved to see that a long, gentle ramp led up to the front door beside the more traditional steps.

Parking the van, he rolled his chair to the rear, opened the doors and operated the hand control which would lower him to the ground. After booking in he was shown to a pleasant, sunny room with lots of space to manoeuvre his chair. He began to relax. His forays into the Peaks would be all the more exciting from a comfortable base like this.

After a very pleasant dinner, served by dining room staff who took no special interest in his chair, (as he was one of three others in similar circumstances) he returned to his room and climbed into bed. He was tired from the long drive.

It was some time, however, before sleep overcame the excitement of the last few days. He slipped away at last, from reality into a dream world, where the roe deer ran and Robin Hood, with his mentor, Herne the Hunter, travelled together to ensure the safety of their wild world.

The next morning was overcast with a threat of rain in the air, but occasional breaks in the cloud showed blue sky, giving David reason to suppose that the day's weather could improve. After breakfast he gathered the picnic hamper he had ordered the night before from the hotel's chef, loaded it into the van and set off to visit some of the places he remembered from his childhood holiday.

First on his list was the farmhouse where he and his family had stayed. After a long, bumpy climb, he was disappointed to find that it had fallen into disuse and was now little more than a crumbling ruin. It was a strange feeling to sit on the edge of that particular moor once again, and to let his eye roam over the familiar sights. He had seen them almost daily in his imagination since he had left to return home from his Peak District holiday, and he was pleased to find that nothing much had changed.

There was the gateway to the moor that Herne had stood by when David had first seen him, and the huge cross on the rocky outcrop above the town which spread over the valley floor below. Memories flooded back and David searched the tree line below for any sign of the weird curtain of multicoloured light which had always seemed to herald Herne's appearance.

Nothing moved, and after a few more moments David disappointedly started the engine and turned the van in the little walled paddock which opened off the lane. He set off back down the long track through the trees to the main road.

'Right!' he thought. 'On to the Goyt Valley, I'm on the right road and almost halfway there.'

The thought of the two weeks he had to spend in this wild, unspoiled part of the Pennine Chain cheered him and dispelled his disappointment almost immediately.

The way to the local beauty spot was well signposted and quite busy. Cars full of people, family groups, middle aged couples and occasionally several teenagers, were all winding

73

The Goyt Valley

sp.

their way down the narrow road which cut its way across and down the steep valley side. The view from the top of the hill was impressive. Across the valley the opposite steep hillside was densely wooded with fir, larch and spruce trees growing close together in great swaths of variegated greens.

Water filled the valley bottom in two separate lakes at different levels. Two huge dams divided and contained the water, each with a road built across between high walls. The road that David was following, crossed the central, dividing dam and continued for a short way up the opposite hillside before turning to run along the water's edge for some considerable distance. A large car park had been constructed on the opposite side of the road, and from here visitors could choose from a network of country pathways which threaded their way through the wooded area and around the lakes.

As David pulled in and parked the van, as near to the water's edge as possible, the threatening cloud cover seemed to split apart and roll back to reveal a blue sky and a brilliant warm sun. David gasped. The leaden, uninteresting water turned in the blinking of an eye to a sparkling shining blue and what, before, appeared to have been cold, wind-driven waves became shining jewels which rushed across the surface of the water.

He reached down his binoculars from the rack above the dashboard where they were stored, next to the citizen's band radio which he had installed for emergencies, and which would make him feel less isolated when he took the van into inaccessible places. He swept the glasses slowly across the surface of the lake in search of any unusual water birds, but could see only a small flock of mallard ducks and several small sailing dinghies from the club house on the opposite bank.

His scrutiny continued until a sudden flash of gold in the sun much nearer to him caught his attention. He swung the binoculars back to bring into focus whatever it was he had seen, and suddenly found himself gazing into the face of one of the prettiest girls he had ever seen. As her long fair hair caught the sunlight it seemed to throw shards of gold in every direction and her brown eyes appeared huge in the binocular's lens.

David only had time for a fleeting, but very strong impression of familiarity before he realized that he was staring at very close quarters, and that the girl had very obviously noticed him. She strode across the car park, her waxed cotton jacket flying open in the breeze of her passing and her hiking boots making a solid clumping sound on the tarmac. David pressed the switch which would wind down the window and smiled apologetically.

'I am sorry for staring at you,' he began haltingly, 'I was looking at the water, er for birds, you know... when I realized I was looking at you instead,' he finished lamely. He risked a glance at the girl's face and was not reassured, she appeared to be more cross than ever.

'I really am very sorry for being rude,' he began again. 'I feel sure I know you, or that I have seen you before somewhere. But I can't think where that might be, and I'm sure that if I had I would remember exactly. Oh dear! I'm rambling, aren't I?'

He looked up again to find that the person in front of him was shaking with laughter at his stumbling efforts to explain himself. She thrust her hand through the open window and said, 'It really is very strange, but I have the same feeling too. I'm Marion by the way, Marion Baker, and I am here on holiday. I have only just arrived and I think the whole area is wonderful. Do you live in the Peak District or are you just visiting too? Oh!' A look of mock horror crossed her face and she pressed her hand to her mouth. 'I seem to be rambling on a bit too!' she laughed gaily. 'It must be catching.'

David laughed with her.

'I was just going for a walk by the water,' she said. 'Would you like to come with me?'

'Very much, if you don't mind me slowing you up a bit,' smiled David, and rolling his chair to the back of the van he operated the lift and appeared grinning, from the rear. Marion was blushing furiously.

'I didn't realize you were disabled,' she said. 'I'm sorry. I should have noticed.'

'Never mind,' replied David. 'I would still like very much to join you in your walk, if you really don't mind. My chair will be fine on the road surface and if you decide to strike off on one of the paths, I'll come back.'

They walked and talked until they reached the end of the lake. Marion sat down on a seat at the water's edge and David pulled his wheelchair up level with the end of the bench.

Marion had just finished her second year as a History student at Oxford University and so they had endless interests and experiences in common. After sitting for an hour or so chatting like old friends, David suddenly remembered his picnic hamper, packed away in the locker in the back of the van, and immediately began to feel hungry. He invited Marion to join him for lunch and they set off back to the car park as fast as they could as hunger overtook them both.

David wished that the meal could go on for ever. He had always been very conscious of his disability, making him rather shy when it came to talking to the girls he knew at home and in the college. Strangely, with Marion he felt completely at home and free to express himself. When the food had all been shared and the empty containers repacked into the hamper, Marion reluctantly told him that she must go.

It was obvious to both of them that they should meet again, and so they arranged to have dinner together that night. David gave Marion the name of his hotel and invited her to eat there with him. She accepted gladly before crossing the car park to her car, a small Fiat four wheel drive, David noticed with interest. She drove off with a wave to find herself a camp site to settle into.

As David locked the chair into position behind the wheel, he glanced up across the dam and his eyes followed the rapidly climbing small car up the steep road. He smiled at the nervous flutter he felt in his stomach when he thought of Marion, and at the pleasure their simple meal together in the sunshine had given him.

David's were not the only eyes which watched the car's ascent. High over the hills which ringed the shining stretch of water, a huge eagle stared down with eyes which shone with an intelligence and a warmth that was unusual in one of its cruel breed.

Snake Pass to Derwent

Dinner the night before had been an experience which David would never forget. Marion had found him sitting in the window of the lounge of the hotel, looking out on to the car park, actually wondering whether she would come or not. They had chatted easily throughout the meal and for several hours afterwards. They were both amazed when the manager had appeared to ask if they would require any further service as it was past midnight and he was going to bed.

They had hurriedly arranged to meet the next morning to take a trip together down the Snake Pass, the famous road through the Pennine mountains which leads into the Hope Valley past the Derwent dam.

They were now driving slowly down the winding road into the valley. The hills on either side soared upward, seeming to bruise the sky with their blunt, rounded summits which rose out of the tree covered lower slopes like a group of monks with newly shaved tonsures.

Soon they began to see bright flashes of light through the trees which lined the road, as sunlight was reflected back from water and after a couple more miles the road began to level out as it ran beside the rapidly widening stream. David turned the van left, off the main road and followed a narrower road which was signposted to Derwent. The way rose and fell gently as it crossed the slopes of the small side valleys, which fed their streams into the main body of water that was the huge Derwent reservoir.

The countryside was dramatically beautiful. Evergreen trees of many kinds swept down to the water's edge, leaving a small rocky beach where the winter water level had scoured the land free of any vegetation. Here and there the edge of the lake rose up to form a rocky promontory. Picnic areas and visitors' photography sites had been established on these higher vantage points.

'It is hard to imagine that most of this has been landscaped by man, isn't it?' said Marion. David smiled, he had been admiring the magnificent views whilst thinking very much the same thing.

'The valley must have been very different before it was flooded,' he said. 'The people in Manchester and Sheffield need the water which is supplied from here, but it is hard to justify flooding an area like this.'

As they talked, they had been approaching the entrance to a narrow unmade lane which ran off at an angle up the hill to their left, away from the water. David reached down to the second gear lever by his side and dropped the van into four wheel drive.

'I have been dying to try this out,' he grinned, as Marion's face took on a fairly worried expression. Gunning the engine he set the van to climbing the steep, rutty track.

The vehicle bounced alarmingly over the deep ridges which ran diagonally across its path where water, cascading off the mountain, had cut deep into the sandstone bedrock of the lane. The van's performance was all that David had hoped for.

In a short time it had carried them away from the other cars and people who lined the edge of the reservoir, transporting them to a quiet clearing in the trees far above, where only the foresters and an occasional shepherd came in the course of their daily work. Marion climbed down to the short, springy turf of the glade and took a deep breath.

'I feel as if I have come home,' she sighed. 'I have lived in the city for most of this life, and yet I feel as if I will always be a stranger there.'

David turned his head quickly to look at her from where he was sitting, looking out of the windscreen at the view of the water spread out below them.

'You said, "this life". What did you mean?' he asked.

Marion blushed. It was much too early in their relationship to tell him about the strange dreams and feelings she had always had, about other lives and other times she was sure that she had shared in. She was convinced that David would think her strange or even mad if she tried to explain the memories of other people's lives which seemed to live in her head alongside the very recent experiences of Marion Baker. In fact she had never been sure how to explain them even to herself, and it was far too important that David thought well of her to take any risks with their new friendship.

'It was just a slip of the tongue,' she replied to his question, with an embarrassed smile. 'Are you going to sit in there all day? It really is wonderful out here, and I am sure I can see a heron down there at the waterside.'

'I am sure your eyes are not that good!' laughed David, nevertheless emerging off the lift a few seconds later, with his binoculars slung around his neck.

The midday sun was bright as it shone down into the clearing, and they headed naturally to the edge of the trees to sit in the shade, saying very little. The companiable silence had gone on for some time with David searching the trees and water below with his glasses, and occasionally exclaiming excitedly when he sighted something of interest. Marion lay by the side of his wheelchair, her back leaning against the huge bole of a fir tree, reading a book she had taken from her bag in the van. She looked up and David's attention was drawn from the countryside to her face as he heard her sharp intake of breath.

He let his eyes follow her pointing finger and there, sweeping through the trees towards them was a dancing, sparkling curtain of multi-coloured light. A dark silhouette seemed to hang in front of this curtain.

Turning and weaving in the air to avoid the trees, the shape of a great bird rushed directly at them, seeming to race the light as it dropped lower and lower towards the grass on the edge of the clearing. David threw his arms around Marion's shoulders and bent over to protect her from the cruel claws which he had seen fleetingly extended forward as the eagle neared the ground. At the same time the strange curtain of light rushed past them, winking out of existence as it did so.

David raised his head. His heart was singing with a joy that he could not contain. His bubbling laughter rang out through

80

the woods, disturbing small birds and animals and startling a flock of wood pigeons into explosive wing clapping flight from the trees higher up on the mountainside. Marion was still suffering from the sight of the eagle, apparently attacking them for no reason. White faced and shaking, she looked up in amazement into David's laughing visage.

'He is here. It must have been Herne all the time!' David cried. Reaching out to shake her shoulders with obvious glee and spinning his chair, he stared into the trees behind them.

Marion turned with him and found she was looking into a pair of the kindest eyes she had ever seen. They belonged to a tall man who was standing against the trunk of the tree she had been leaning against. He was dressed in a tunic and leggings of a sacking-like material, and on his head he wore what at first appeared to Marion to be a headdress of antlers.

She had seen this being before. Many times in her dreams and borrowed memories she had met and talked with him. As he stood before them now she knew without doubt that this was Herne the Hunter, and that she had lived those lives and those experiences in other times because she was in some way connected to him.

Herne spoke. 'Greetings to you both,' he said. 'I trust my travelling form did not alarm you too much. The eagle is swift, and sees all from his great height. I find it useful to borrow his wings every now and then.'

David could hardly contain his feelings. He had been quite close to convincing himself that the adventures he remembered sharing with this extraordinary being in his childhood had been wishes rather than reality. Now, however, he was sure this was not so. Herne had returned, and David knew that his coming must herald a new episode in his life as Herne's Champion.

Champions Both!

Herne moved away from the tree and sat down, crossing his long legs at the ankles and placing his elbows on his upraised knees.

'There is work to do for my Champions,' he said. 'As you two have travelled together through all the ages of man, so you must be together now to protect my Kingdom from his greed.' He turned to David. 'You were just a boy when we last met,' he said. 'But I showed you then some ways that my Champions had lived in the past, and I told you that you would be my Champion in this age. You have started well with your writing and your concern for the wild places of the world. I am pleased with the work you have done.

'And you Marion,' he turned again and Marion noticed that what she had thought to be a headdress was in fact a magnificent pair of antlers growing from Herne's head. He smiled kindly at her.

'I have guided your path through life for more years than I care to remember. You too have been my Champion in ages past. Your mind has always retained parts of those other lives and your service to my kingdom, but now the time has come for you to act together in this age of the world.

'A small part of my kingdom is in danger. I can tell you no more than that. You must discover the problem for yourselves. The solution must be rooted in this age for the remedy to have any lasting effect on the world. I can only help you a little, when your need is greatest. Now I must leave you, but look long at the valley below when I have gone. It will give you the first clue that you will need.'

As Herne spoke the last few words, he threw out his arm to

point down into the valley, and the eyes of the two young people instinctively followed. The view was completely different. There was no large stretch of water. Instead, the valley sides dropped steeply for a much greater distance until they almost met on the banks of a fast flowing, tumbling river. David turned back to where Herne had stood, a question on his lips.

'When is this?' he began, but the glade was empty. Herne had gone, vanished as if he had never been there at all.

David spun back to continue his scrutiny of the valley below them. The firs seemed to have disappeared to be replaced by smooth hillsides covered in rough moorland grass, heather and bracken. Lower down the valley stood a village, a small group of cottages clustered round a solid gritstone church with a high Norman spire. Away on the opposite hillside, just above the village, a rather grand house stood, surrounded by tall trees and rhododendron bushes. David turned with shining eyes to where Marion knelt on the soft grass, reaching out to clasp her shoulders with trembling hands.

'No wonder I've felt like we have been friends for ever,' he said softly. 'You have been my companion through many adventures. You were Maid Marion when I was Robin Hood, Alice De Lud Auk when I was Henry Montain, and I don't doubt for a minute that we have shared other lives together in our service to Herne.' Marion rocked forward and kissed him on the forehead.

'I have known for years that something was missing from my life, and now at last I know what it is. When we have time we must talk about our pasts and our future, but for now we should follow Herne's advice.' David nodded, rolling his chair to the edge of the clearing and staring down on the unfamiliar scene.

'What has happened?' whispered Marion. 'What has he done to the water?'

David took her hand reassuringly. He had seen what Herne could do with time before. 'Don't worry,' he said. 'I think Herne has sent us back to a time when the Derwent was a river running down this valley, before the dams were built. That must be Derwent village and the house on the hill, Derwent Hall. They were buried when the dam was built.'

Village life seemed to be going on as it always had. A dappled grey horse trotted smartly up the main street carrying a well dressed young man towards the Hall. The children playing tag in the street and the old men who sat and gossiped outside the doorway of the public house touched their forelocks or raised their caps as he passed.

From their elevated position on the hillside, David and Marion could see several women hanging clothing out to dry on the lines which ran the length of each garden, behind the cottages that lined the road. Several small shops were interspersed throughout the cottages giving the impression that they too had been dwellings until their owners had decided to try their hands at shopkeeping. A grocers, a butchers and a bakers all stood with their doors open to their customers and small groups of women, baskets over their arms, stood chatting outside each door.

A little way down the valley, on the bank of the rushing churning Derwent stood a mill, the large water wheel turning slowly. Several horses, firmly fixed into the shafts of their carts, were tethered outside and small black and white sheepdogs chased each other in and out of their huge muscular legs, showing no concern for the iron shod hooves which could have crushed them effortlessly.

Men were unloading bags of grain and carrying them into the mill, whilst others reloaded bags of flour onto the empty drays. Their rough, good humoured banter carried to the watchers on the still warm air, and David smiled as he realized that he could understand little of the thick country accents.

Suddenly, the whole world seemed to shudder. David and Marion turned to each other in surprise and when the two startled youngsters looked back into the village the scene in front of them had changed again.

Far down the valley a monstrous wall had appeared, and the land on both banks of the river was rutted and broken where heavy, wheeled transport had passed to and fro continually for some considerable time. Marion shivered.

'Do you see anything odd about the village?' she whispered softly. 'There are no people. The whole place is deserted.'

David nodded. 'I was thinking the same thing,' he said.

84

The Derwent Dam

85

'Herne must have shifted time again. We are seeing the village now after the people have been moved away. That wall down there is the dam.'

The air in the valley bottom shivered like the mirage effect which turns tarmac to water on a hot summer's day. The neglected, abandoned flowers in the cottage gardens seemed to wilt and grow old as they watched.

'Time is speeding up,' gasped Marion. 'Just like running a film on fast forward.'

David grasped her hand tightly. 'Look at the water,' he croaked, the lump in his throat making talking at all very difficult. The river had begun to back up behind the dam wall and was filling the bottom of the valley rapidly.

The scene darkened through an incredibly rapid dusk to a full dark, and to David's amazement the moon rose, crossed the sky and set again in a matter of moments. As they watched a pale sun rose over the hill behind them and spun over the valley before dropping out of sight behind the other hillside. All the time the water was rising. The sun and moon followed each other in their courses at an ever increasing rate until it was impossible to see which was which, and the light and dark of the passing days became a dull grey, uniform light.

The mill was flooded first. Wooden bin lids and barrels floated out of the doors and windows, surrounded by a dreadful greyish white scum of hundreds of years of flour dust. The village vanished quite quickly after that. The encroaching, all enveloping water seeming to sweep in through the ground floor windows and doors, only to burst out through the bedroom windows and chimney pots carrying with it a terrible mess of forgotten or abandoned household articles and rubbish.

There was a pause while the dark forbidding waters spread over the widening section of the valley, and a final rush which consumed the Hall and the church spire. Time seemed then to slow and return to its natural flow as the air shimmered around them once again and the peaceful Derwent Valley returned to the present, giving no indication of what lay below the surface.

David looked at Marion's shocked pale face and thought that he was probably looking much the same. After a little while had passed Marion spoke. Her voice shook with emotion and she managed to control it with difficulty.

'How many homes did that water destroy?' she asked of nobody in particular. 'Not only the people but the thousands of wild animals and birds which lived down there were made homeless, and some at least will have been drowned.'

They climbed slowly into the van, all the while looking down on the placid water of the Derwent which now, to them seemed menacing and cold. They had passed through two small villages below the dam wall and were well on their way to the village of Hope when David voiced the question which had been bothering them both.

'What could Herne have meant by showing us that bit of the past?' he wondered. 'Is it going to happen again, now, in our time? I'm sure that if it were then people would know, and some at least would be protesting. A thing like that would be all over the national news.'

'There must have been a reason though,' replied Marion. 'Herne told us it was a clue, and that part of his domain was threatened. Perhaps we can find something which will help in the local newspaper. We can buy one as we go through Buxton on the way back to the hotel.'

Marion had left her car in the hotel car park that morning and the two went in for afternoon tea when they arrived. They spent a fruitless hour checking the newspaper for any clue to their puzzle, but eventually had to give up and admit defeat. They were no wiser now than when Herne had left them on the hill above Derwent water.

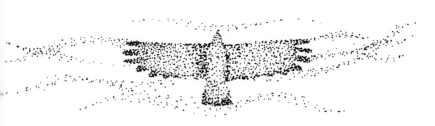

Lost on the Moor

David woke up with a start. The room was dark and seemed to throb with a deep moaning sound. As he lay, only half awake and trying to gather his scattered wits, the bedroom was lit by a bright white flash of light, which threw the furniture into stark relief.

The lightning left him temporarily blinded for a few seconds but, nevertheless put his mind at rest. The eerie sound which had woken him was the wind, he realized, blowing through the eaves of the hotel, buffeting and pushing at his window as if it wanted to be let in.

David chuckled to himself at the thought, and wriggled a little lower into the warm, comfortable bed. He knew these summer storms could strike without warning up here in the mountains, and that it would pass quickly. Sleep was once again claiming his heavy eyelids when a new thought entered his head, which made him sit upright with a jerk.

'Marion is sleeping in a small tent in the middle of a field in this weather,' he thought. 'I hope she is all right.' After a few more moments he realized that there was nothing he could do in the middle of the night and went back to sleep with a vague, warm feeling of satisfaction at having someone to care about underlying his concern.

He need not have worried. Marion had pulled back the flap of her tiny lightweight tent and was curled up snugly in her sleeping bag watching the storm lash the trees alongside the campsite. She was filled with a feeling of excitement and pleasure she had rarely experienced before. For the first time she was aware of a sense of purpose in her life.

Herne's words to her the day before had struck Marion

88

with a force equal to that of the wind which was now challenging the mighty strength of the mature sycamores and elms. She was convinced that her life would never be the same again. There was an elemental force in the storm which seemed akin to the newly awakened emotions within herself.

The next day dawned cool and overcast. Occasional showers of fat, overweight raindrops splattered down, filling gutters and drains to overflowing as the storm was bounced from mountain top to mountain top across the deep dales and high, open moorland.

The talk of the guests at breakfast was of very little but the weather and the storm of the night before. David was just deciding to have another piece of toast, when the hotel manager showed Marion into the dining room and seated her at David's table.

'Good morning,' she greeted him. 'The thought of cooking my breakfast in the tent in this weather didn't appeal at all, and so I thought I would come and join you. I hope you don't mind?'

The two young people smiled shyly at each other, Herne's revelations had produced an odd feeling between them. They were still relative strangers in reality and yet they felt drawn together and at ease in each other's company.

David talked, quietly and easily, as Marion ate her breakfast. He told her about his family and his home, about his hopes and dreams for the future and about his adventures as Herne's Champion here in the Peak District when he was twelve years old. Presently they drifted from the dining room to the inglenook by the fire in the lounge, and Marion told David about her life before she had decided, on the spur of the moment, to visit Derbyshire in her vacation.

The weather showed no sign of clearing and so David and Marion decided to take the van for a ride over the Cat and Fiddle road, named after the very famous public house which stands at the highest point of the road between Buxton and the nearby small town of Macclesfield, where Marion had heard of a silk museum which she wanted to visit. The views over the Cheshire plain, which spread out before them like a carpet as they dropped down off the hills, were spectacular although the dark, low cloud obscured the distant horizon and any view of the Welsh Mountains.

By late afternoon they had exhausted the possibilities for entertainment in the town and took the road towards Stockport. They intended to make a large circle before re-entering the Peak District via Glossop, Hayfield and the dark bulk of Kinder Scout, the highest of the region's mountains.

David took a road out of Stockport which he was sure would lead them towards Kinder, but at each successive crossroads he grew less and less sure of his direction. They were soon climbing ever higher, on rapidly deteriorating roads. They came out onto a bleak and windswept moor as what little light the dull, stormy day had produced darkened into dusk.

'I think you had better stop for a minute,' said Marion, 'whilst we try to get our bearings.' David pulled the van over to the side of the track in response and turned off the ignition.

As the sound of the engine died away, they became aware of a deep rumbling noise which seemed to be coming from behind them. As they turned in their seats to stare out of the rear windows of the van, a large truck, it's lights blazing, breasted the crest of the hill and bore down on them. David barely had time to restart the engine and pull the van completely off the road, before the truck swept past, making the van shake with the nearness of its passing.

'He seems to know where he's going,' laughed David. 'Let's follow him for a while and see if we can't find our way back to a more main road. I daren't try to turn here anyway. The moor looks pretty wet and I would hate to get the van into a peat bog.'

They followed the lorry for several miles, but just as they were beginning to wonder if it would ever stop, it vanished. They had been driving over relatively flat moorland, following the bright tail lights of the truck, when in the blink of an eye, there was nothing in front of them at all.

Marion's cry of surprise had hardly left her lips when the van tipped sharply forward to begin the descent of a steep hill, which dropped away in front of them, falling quickly past high rocky walls on both sides of the road.

90

'He must have switched off his lights as he went over the brow of the hill,' reasoned David. 'I wonder why?'

Switching his own lights to full beam, he increased speed as much as he dared, but could see no trace of the truck or its lights.

'The driver must have turned off the track up ahead,' said Marion, straining her eyes through the windscreen. 'Yes, there! Look, there's a cleft in the rock and a lane leads away through it to the left. It looks very well used. I wonder where it goes!'

David stopped the van on the grass by the side of the turning and reversed very carefully into it.

'It seems very steep. I don't think it would be wise to go any further,' he said. 'Perhaps we had better go back the way we came.'

They had climbed back to the moor when another truck appeared out of the darkness, forcing them to leave the road again as it went past. David was glad of the four wheel drive capability of his vehicle, but nevertheless was angry with the inconsiderate way in which the two truck drivers had behaved.

'What on earth can they be doing up here at this time of night?' he wondered aloud and glancing across at Marion was surprised to see a strange expression on her face. A puzzled look was slowly being replaced by a look of comprehension.

'Perhaps it wasn't an accident that brought us this way tonight,' she said. 'Were we brought here to see exactly what we did see? Could this be another clue from Herne to help us in the quest?'

'It's possible,' replied David excitedly. 'I said yesterday that people would know if something was going on, but I doubt if that is true up here. We must be miles from anywhere.'

'Not quite anywhere!' Marion pointed across the dark moor. 'There is a light over there. It must be a farm. What a remote place to live. I think we should come back here tomorrow, in daylight, and have a better look at that mysterious valley.'

The Hidden Valley

The moors presented a completely different aspect the next morning. The sun was shining in a clear blue sky. No trace of the storm remained, everywhere wild flowers blossomed amongst the dark green heather and the fresh, vibrant bracken. It was difficult to believe that they were following the same track as the night before. David and Marion began to feel that perhaps the darkness and the weather had contributed rather a lot to their suspicions.

'We must be quite near now,' said Marion. 'Yes, that must be the farm we saw the lights in last night.' She pointed away to where a group of buildings huddled under the lee of a gently rising slope on the horizon, which ended abruptly in a rocky crag dropping in a sheer face back to the moor.

They had driven just a few yards more when the roar of a powerful diesel engine penetrated the cab of the van. Looking in the rear view mirror, David saw a heavy lorry approaching them. The driver flashed his lights and David pulled the van over onto the grass verge. As the huge truck passed them, they were surprised to see the driver and his mate smiling down at them and waving their thanks for David's prompt action.

'That makes a pleasant change from the drivers of those trucks we saw last night,' grinned David. 'It is hard to believe that anything sinister is going on when you see it all in daylight.'

Before they reached the place where the road dipped into the valley, they had seen several empty waggons coming towards them from the opposite direction. They had been passed by two more, fully laden, coming up behind.

'All these trucks are full of soil and gravel,' Marion mused slowly. 'Whilst I'm sure that the one we saw last night was a flat bedded lorry with its load stacked under a tarpaulin. Perhaps they are going to different places.'

David let his eyes wander across the flat, empty moor.

'I can't see where any of them could be going up here,' he said. 'I have never seen such an empty expanse of land in all my life.'

The van tipped forward as it ran over the crest of the hill, holding no fears or surprise now for its occupants. They could see in the sunlight that they were entering a steep valley, which, judging by its wide, rounded bottom, had been cut through the rock countless centuries ago by the slow, ponderous passage of an icy glacier, rather than by the small stream which now meandered down by the side of the road.

David parked the van at the top of the slope and they looked with interest down into the valley. The slopes on the right hand side were grass covered and rounded in appearance, while on the left great humps of dark rock stuck out from the steep banks to form a craggy wall, which in places reached all the way from the valley bottom to the rim of the moor above.

Suddenly, the blunt nose of a truck appeared to grow from the solid rock at the point where David had turned the van the night before, and the sound of a labouring engine echoed up the valley. The rest of the vehicle followed, turning towards them up the hill, as it pulled slowly out of the narrow rocky defile through which the lane ran. When it was past and the sound of its motor had receded over the edge of the moor, David eased the van forward to the turning and crept slowly in.

The track was deeply covered in thick glutinous mud but a solid base of bedrock allowed the fat, chunky tyres to grip. The steep rock face on either side of them continued for a few hundred feet, twisting and turning through its course. As they approached the place where the rock opened out, they were amazed to discover that they were looking down into another valley very similar in character to the one they had just left. They could see from their elevated vantage point that the valley appeared to be scooped out of the high edge of the moorland. The track climbed quite steeply at its far end before finally crossing a saddle-like depression in the skyline.

Below them, the valley was a hive of activity. Towards the far end the grass covered slopes and rock outcrops ran down to another small stream and the narrow grassy banks on either side were relatively unspoiled, but nearer to where they sat the lovely natural lines of the valley walls were ruined. The bottom of the valley was being filled in.

Huge earthmoving machines were spreading load after load of dirt and broken rock across the valley floor to raise, and so widen, the flat base area. As the high wall of rubble moved down the valley, pipes had been laid to carry the water from the stream underground.

Where the valley had been filled to a depth almost level with the place where the track ran over the saddle in front of them, a cluster of wooden huts and sheds had been erected, obviously for use as stores and rest rooms for the men who were working all over the site.

David turned to Marion where she sat staring out at the scene of desolation which was being created in this hidden peaceful place, and whispered softly, 'I don't think we need to look any further for the answer to Herne's puzzle. This valley is being filled and changed just like the Derwent. Only this one is being filled with rubble instead of water. Someone must be intending to build here.'

Marion nodded sadly.

'Yes,' she answered. 'But I can't think what we can do to stop it. Assuming that whoever the developer is he has all the relevant permission from the authorities, then there is nothing that we can do.'

'That would seem to be a good place to start then,' rejoined David. 'We can at least ask the Town Hall for a look at the planning application,'

As he had been speaking, he had been watching a Landrover begin the long climb up the winding road from the huts to where they sat. Now he became worried that strangers might not be welcome here.

He put his van into reverse and began to negotiate the winding way back through the rocky cleft. It was slow going but they were still a long way ahead of the labouring jeep, when the van pulled out from behind the high walls into the wider valley beyond. David breathed a sigh of relief as he turned his head to the front and massaged his aching neck muscles with his free hand.

They were climbing slowly up the edge of the moor when Marion gave a gasp of surprise. A large tractor was slowing to a stop on the road above them, its squat widespread front wheels and bulbous headlights giving it the appearance of a giant, menacing insect.

The road was completely, and David guessed deliberately, blocked. He began to swing the wheel into the first manoeuvre of a three point turn, but as he did so the Landrover shot out of the entrance to the lane below and screeched to a halt across the road. They were trapped.

A small, roughly dressed man climbed down from the cab of the tractor. His once smart tweed sportscoat, green with age, was tied around his middle with a piece of baler twine and the heavy wellington boots he wore on his feet were caked in mud and manure. He sauntered down the hill towards the van, while a man in overalls walked up from the back of the Landrover. David rolled down his window as the two met by the door of the van, but they both ignored him completely for a few moments. The tractor driver spoke to his companion.

'What have we here then?' he sneered. 'A couple of tourists? Or,' his voice dropped to a menacing hiss, 'a couple of snoopers?' The other man shrugged.

'I don't know, Sid,' he replied. 'We spotted them on the track to the site, and came up to see what they were doing. But they couldn't have seen anything from up here.'

Sid lashed out with a blow to the man's midriff, and he doubled over, gasping for breath.

'I would shut up if I were you,' he muttered coldly. 'I'm sure Mr Roper wouldn't be pleased to hear you talking about "things to see" in front of snoopers.'

He turned to speak to David and Marion with a sly smile, which never quite seemed to touch his cold, calculating eyes.

'This is private property, young man, I'm sure you wouldn't want to trespass on my land, now would you?' he said. 'I don't know what you were doing down in the valley, but it is very dangerous down there for members of the public with all that heavy machinery about. So I don't want to see you in these parts again.'

The smile slipped from his face to be replaced by a near snarl.

'You do understand, don't you?' he repeated softly, his face thrust very close to David's through the window of the van. 'It could be very, very dangerous.'

David nodded wordlessly, and Sid swaggered off up the road to his tractor, confident that he had frightened off the young couple and that they would keep away from his farm, and the hidden valley for a long time to come.

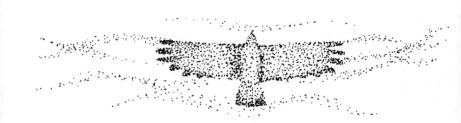

Growing Suspicions

'It seems to me,' mused Marion that there must be something odd going on, if not downright illegal. Why else would they try to frighten us like that?'

David grinned. 'I don't know about "try", he laughed. 'They certainly frightened me!'

'We can't give up now though,' Marion replied. 'I am sure this is what Herne wanted us to find, and if he did, then it stands to reason that there must be something we can do to stop it.'

They were comfortably ensconced, David in his wheelchair and Marion in a camp chair by the side of her tent. The discussion had carried them through the afternoon and into the evening.

Marion had cooked them both a meal on the tiny stove outside the door of her small tent, while David had kept a kettle constantly on the boil on the cooker in the van, to make the endless cups of coffee which had lubricated their deliberations.

They had been for the last hour, however, getting very little further. They had studied the ordinance survey map of the area and thought they had found the name of the farm on the moor. It was called Underhill, presumably because of its position beneath the long rise in the moorland.

They had decided that they could identify the hidden valley for the purpose of asking at the planning office for permission to see the planning application. Though really that was all they could do until the Council Offices opened the next morning.

'Why don't we go for a drive?' suggested David. 'It's a

lovely evening. We could stop for a drink in one of the villages if you like.'

They were soon meandering through the country lanes of the Peak District, enjoying the warm evening sunshine and the magnificent views over the tops of the drystone walls. David laughed suddenly.

'I don't know if this is coincidence,' he said, 'or if I have been subconsciously drifting this way. But up there,' he pointed through the windscreen to where the hills seemed to rise to the sky in front of them, 'is the moor and our hidden valley. Perhaps we should stop in the next village for our drink without going any nearer.'

Marion agreed wholeheartedly. The threatening attitude of the men that afternoon had shaken her more than she cared to admit, and she had no wish to meet them again.

They soon entered a small hamlet, each grey stone cottage facing onto a green with a large pond in the centre. A group of children were playing cricket in the failing light, reluctant to admit that the long summer's day was over.

To one side of the green stood a public house, its frontage much longer and more elaborate than the surrounding dwellings, although its grey slate roof followed the same low line. David was struck by an impression that all the buildings were hunched up, their backs turned to the weather. He could imagine them half buried in piled snow as the cruel wind carried the blizzard down off the moor.

'It would be wonderful to be up here in the winter,' he thought, 'when the visitors had gone home. Every cottage and pub would sport a blazing log fire and the local people would spend the time telling stories of past winters and greater snowfalls.' He filed the thought away for future reference and turned the van into the car park behind the King's Head.

'Let me out here,' smiled Marion. 'I'll go and see if there is room for us. I hate a smokey, crowded room, don't you?'

She slipped from the van and went in through the front door. David continued round the side of the building and parked the van. He smiled to himself as he thought how tactful Marion was being. He knew she had really gone to check that he could get his wheelchair into the building and that the landlord wouldn't object. Some did on the grounds that the chair took up too much room or blocked the space between tables. He was grateful that she had tried not to remind him of his disability.

He was just wheeling the chair off the hoist as she emerged from a side door and waved him over.

'There is a really snug little lounge with hardly anyone in it,' she called. 'It's just perfect for us.'

David ordered drinks and the landlord brought them over to their table. He chatted for a few minutes before another customer, in the public bar, called him over to serve them. Marion and David settled down with their drinks and were soon deep in conversation.

After a little while, they became aware of a raucous voice, raised boastfully in the other room. They glanced nervously at each other.

'I'm sure I know that voice,' whispered David.

'I don't think I will ever be able to forget it,' replied Marion. 'It's Sid, the farmer, and he sounds a bit worse for wear.'

'I've worked all my life up on that moor,' Sid was saying, his drunken voice rising and carrying clearly to the two young people in the lounge. 'Soon I'll be able to get away from here and go and live somewhere where farming is easier.'

A low mumble followed as if whoever he was speaking to had asked a question.

'Never you mind. It's none of your business where I'll get the money from,' Sid answered the unheard question. 'I've done a deal with some city friends of mine that'll make me rich. Why should I care about the folks round here? They never give me the time of day.'

There was a crash as a chair fell over in the public bar, shortly followed by another as the door into the lounge burst open, banging against its hinges. Sid stood, swaying in the doorway, leering at them drunkenly. David tensed and reaching across the table took Marion's hand to reassure her.

They waited for Sid to recognize them but, after staring rudely for a few moments he turned away, muttering darkly about "ruddy tourists" and crashed out of the front door of the inn. They saw him from the window of the lounge stumble across the road and climb unsteadily into a dilapidated old van, which he drove away, smoking and shuddering, up the road in the direction of the moor and his farm.

'Whew!' grinned David, giving Marion's hand an extra squeeze. 'That was close! Thank goodness he hadn't parked that dreadful old van in the car park. He couldn't have failed to recognize ours, even in the state he was in.'

The landlord came through into the lounge and stopped by their table.

'I'm dreadfully sorry,' he apologized. 'He's a real nuisance is Sid when he gets too much to drink, which is, I'm sorry to say, quite often. I wish he wouldn't come in here really, but mine is the only pub for miles around, and his farm is up on the moor above the village.'

David saw a chance to check that the information they had gleaned from the map was correct.

'Would that be Underhill farm?' he asked, trying to sound casual.

'That's right,' the landlord grinned. 'It's been in his family for generations but he doesn't seem to make much of it. My father was landlord here before me, and he used to talk of great flocks of sheep up there on the moor, all belonging to the Berisfords of Underhill. But now I hardly know how Sid Berisford makes enough money to drink the way he does.'

Marion did her best to look sympathetic. 'He was talking about making a lot of money if I heard him right,' she said. 'Life can't be all bad up there on the moor.'

The landlord shrugged.

'It beats me how he intends to get rich. He has sold off a piece of the land to a developer for quite a considerable sum, I know. But most of that money has gone to pay the debts he has been running up all over the district for years. There will be precious little left when he has paid off everyone he owes money to.'

David looked thoughtful. 'We were up on the moor today,' he said. 'That was when we saw Underhill farm. We kept getting passed by waggons full of rubble. Are they anything to do with Mr Berisford?'

'Oh them!' snorted the landlord. 'Folks round here are sick to death of them. We can't be doing with them coming through the village. They never stop. All day, and sometimes even late at night they come through here on their way up to Underhill. They're carting stuff up to level the valley for building. Although why they have to cart at night, I don't know. They are a darn nuisance, I can tell you.'

The landlord wandered off to gather glasses from the public bar. David and Marion looked at each other.

'Are you thinking what I'm thinking?' said David softly.

'I'm rather afraid that I am,' replied Marion. 'We're going to have to take a closer look at those huts in the valley.'

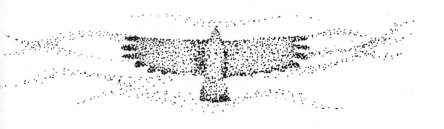

Some Answers, More Questions

David and Marion met the next morning in the car park behind the Council offices. They approached the deeply polished, old mahogany reception desk in the foyer, where portraits of past mayors lined the walls. Some of the earlier ones had great beards or mutton chop whiskers, whilst the more modern were mostly clean shaven. They all wore the ermine trimmed robe and gold chain of their office. Each and every one of them stared down at David and Marion with a stern expression.

David asked for the planning office, feeling all the time as if he should whisper for fear of disturbing the people in the pictures. The receptionist at the desk told him that it was on the first floor. Luckily the building had a good sized lift and David was able to ride up without any trouble.

Once in the outer office of the department they needed, they found the clerical assistant behind the desk very helpful. She knew of the planned development on Underhill Farm and quickly disappeared into a back room to find the relevant file.

While David and Marion were waiting for her to return, the door to an inner office, bearing a plaque marked Director of Planning, opened and a small, overweight man backed out into the room. He was wearing a very old, very baggy, green tweed suit, which looked as if it had been made for an altogether bigger man. Rather bent gold rimmed glasses perched precariously on his bulbous nose and a small, worn hairpiece sat in the middle of a much larger bald spot on his head. He appeared to be almost bowing as he rubbed his hands nervously together. He was talking so fast that all his words seemed to run together.

'I can't thank you enough, James,' he called back into the Director's office. 'I'm sure Mr Roper will be very grateful for all your support.'

He turned away, closing the door behind him and the two young friends could see that he was sweating profusely. He produced a handkerchief from the top of his jacket and began to mop his forehead.

At that moment, the clerical assistant returned, smiling apologetically.

'I really am very sorry,' she said. 'The Director has the Underhill file on his desk at the moment.' She turned as she noticed the other occupant of the office and smiled. 'Oh! Mr Warwick, have you finished your meeting with the Director? Perhaps he will have finished with the file. I'll go and see.' She knocked on the Director's door and waited for him to call come in. A few moments later she was back, the file tucked under her arm.

Mr Warwick had wandered out into the corridor whilst she had been away, and David could see him staring back through the glass wall into the outer office, a worried expression puckering the corners of his faded blue eyes behind the thick lenses of his glasses.

The clerk spread out the file on the counter and produced several official looking documents from it.

'Now,' she said kindly. 'What was it you wanted to know?'

When Marion and David left the office about half an hour later they were in possession of some, at least, of the answers they felt they needed to help unravel the mystery of the hidden valley. The planning application had been submitted by a Mr Warwick, a local architect, presumably the man they had seen leaving, on behalf of a company called Roper Developments Ltd., which seemed to have offices in Manchester and London.

Marion had copied down the address of the Manchester office and the clerk had added the information that Mr Roper, the head of the company, was a very important property developer and that nobody in the planning department had ever seen him. The application was for a time share holiday development which would consist of chalets, grouped around a central recreational area. The detailed plans which were attached to the application papers showed a swimming pool, squash courts, a restaurant with two bars and a small supermarket, making the complex almost self contained in its remote valley high up on the moor. Across each document was stamped the word 'Approved'.

As David and Marion made their way back to the van, they became aware that the architect, Mr Warwick, was lurking under the trees at the edge of the car park. He was obviously waiting for them but not wanting to be seen from the building. As soon as he saw them, he drew further back into the shadows and beckoned frantically.

David rolled his chair over to where he stood followed by Marion.

'What did you want with the Underhill file?' he hissed, looking nervously from side to side, and never letting his eyes rest on the faces of the young couple for more than a split second at a time.

'We were up on the moor near there yesterday, looking round,' replied Marion. David broke in before she could say anything else.

'Yes. We heard you were building a holiday village,' he added quickly. 'We thought we might like to take a couple of weeks a year in one of the chalets. It's in a lovely spot.'

'Oh I see,' answered the heavily perspiring Mr Warwick. 'Well, I don't think that would be a good idea at all. That place could be quite dangerous you know.' David's eyebrows shot up in surprise.

'What do you mean?' he asked, but Mr Warwick was beginning to realize that he had said too much in his efforts to put off this rather nice young couple, and was determined not to make another mistake.

'Oh!' he said airily. 'I don't think the complex will be accessible for disabled people like yourself.' With that, he turned and hurried away through the trees to his car, his baggy green tweed suit flapping around him.

Marion waited until he had climbed into his car and shut the door before asking. 'And what was that all about?' Her shoulders were shaking with suppressed laughter at the strange neglected appearance of the architect.

'I thought you were going to tell him about our suspicions,' mumbled David guiltily, 'and so I got in quickly to stop you. I just said the first thing that came into my head. I am sorry.'

'Not to worry,' laughed Marion. 'No harm done, and I suspect that he did much the same when he was talking about there not being facilities for the disabled. I don't think for a minute that that was what he really meant. But, if it wasn't that, then what did he mean? He appeared to be really scared about something.'

The two set off to look for a cafe in which to have some lunch and to continue their conversation. After a good meal, David rolled his chair back from the table to go over what they knew, and what they suspected, again.

'The planning application is genuine,' he began, 'that much we know, and although we don't like the use the valley will be put to, we can do nothing about it. I do wonder however, how the local people feel about it all. The building work seems to be being done by the property developer's own men, which means that there will be very little extra work for the locals. Even when it is finished and open to the public, it is so self contained that I can't see it contributing much to the local tourism effort. The guests up there will arrive by car or coach, spend all their time in the complex and go home at the end of their holiday. I can't see the local shopkeepers being very pleased with that.

'The architect is a nervous wreck and seems to think that something is wrong in the valley, which is borne out by the way that the men who work there chase away strangers.

'Sid Berisford, the farmer and the former owner of the land, appears to be in collusion with the site workers and is openly boasting about a shady source of big money.

'So! What have we got?'

Marion grimaced painfully. 'I for one, have a headache,' she grinned, 'and very little else. All the facts we know seem to contradict each other. I suggest we take things easy this afternoon and try to slip down into the valley tonight. I think that there is a vital piece of the puzzle that we don't know yet and I'm sure we will find it there.'

The Valley of Death

The moonlight seemed impossibly bright to David and Marion as the van inched its way slowly down off the moor. Marion shivered involuntarily as they passed the place where Sid had blocked the road with his tractor.

'But can we really be sure that there is nobody down on the site?' she asked for the third time since leaving the King's Head in the village far below them. David sighed; he didn't feel as confident as he was trying to appear, but he did feel that they had to get a closer look at the work that was going on in the valley and he couldn't think of any other way of doing it.

'The landlord told us,' he began again, 'that there have been no trucks through the village for a couple of nights and as far as he knows there had never been a nightwatchman up here. I think we should creep very slowly through the entrance to the lane and have a good look first, before going any further. After all, we know we can get out again before anyone from the site can reach us.'

Marion's muttered agreement sounded anything but convinced. However, she kept quiet as the van made the turn into the cleft through the rock and crept very slowly, its engine running hardly above idling speed, down the twisting track. As they approached the last bend before the rocky walls opened out into the valley, Marion held up her hand.

'Stop here for a moment,' she whispered, the tension in the air making her keep her voice low although it was impossible for anyone to overhear her. 'I'll walk forward a little way and check out the site on foot.'

106

Before David could protest she had opened the door and slipped away into the darkness, keeping close to the rock face and staying in the shadows which the slanting moonlight threw over one side of the track.

It seemed like a long time to David before he caught sight of her slipping back through the shadows towards him, and he breathed a sigh of relief.

'Where have you been?' he asked as Marion climbed back into her seat and she turned to him in surprise.

'I've only been gone a few minutes,' she laughed, and David was glad that she couldn't see him blushing in the darkened interior of the van.

'Sorry,' he said quietly. 'I was worried about you. Did you see anything down there? Any lights or workmen moving about?'

'No,' Marion replied. 'I think the landlord was right. There are no lights and the place seems deserted. If we are going to have a look, there will never be a better time.'

David slipped the van into first gear and checked that the four wheel drive lever was engaged. The track was steep and very muddy and he felt that it would take all his driving skill to negotiate it safely. He eased the van round the last bend in the rock and began the long descent. It was far too dangerous to try to follow the winding, rutted track without any lights and so David switched on the dipped headlights with a muttered prayer that there really was no-one in the valley.

The narrow road was cut into the side of the steep hillside, and wound across the almost sheer face in a series of shallow loops with steep, sharp turns at each end. David kept the van as close to the lefthand side of the lane as he possibly could, hugging the rocky wall and avoiding the long, steep drop to the valley bottom. The van's progress was erratic and very uncomfortable for its two passengers. The constant passage of the heavy lorries had cut deep ruts in the lane's surface, and the van's narrower wheelbase meant that only one or other of the sets of wheels were running comparatively smoothly at any time. The other set leapt and bumped across the extremely uneven verge. It was a great relief to them both when the last bend was passed, and the van rolled to a halt by the side of the cluster of huts.

David relaxed back into his seat with a sigh, turning off the engine and the lights.

'Let's give our eyes time to get used to the dark,' he said. 'Then we can have a look around.'

Marion was very relieved to find that her analysis of the situation from the top of the lane appeared to be correct. The huts were all in darkness and nothing stirred across the flat surface of the levelled valley bottom.

'I'll go and have a look,' she said softly, thinking of the difficulty that David would have with his wheelchair, but David did not intend to be left out of this most exciting part of their adventure.

'The surface here looks pretty level,' he argued. 'I'm sure my chair will cope with it.' He rolled the chair to the hoist at the back of the van to forestall any further argument from Marion, and let himself down to the hard gravel surface of the worksite. Marion soon joined him and together they inspected the huts.

Several of them were open fronted garages and store sheds containing all the machinery and equipment normal to any building site, but two were of special interest to the two young people. One was obviously the site office. A quick look through the windows by the light of David's torch showed Marion two desks, a large drawing board with plans pinned to it and a row of filing cabinets lining the back wall.

There was a door in the centre of this wall and Marion realized that the room she could see occupied only two-thirds of the space in the hut. She relayed all this information to David. After trying the door and finding it, as they expected, firmly locked, they moved round to the side of the hut.

The smaller portion of the hut at the back seemed to be a store room of some sort. There was a small door at the far end of it which was secured by a huge brass padlock and where the windows which should have let light into this room were supposed to be there was a panel of strong new wood.

'That must be where they keep any tools and small machinery which they need to keep safe from a sneakthief,' David guessed. 'It would be easy to issue things from there to the men who are working on the site and if everyone has to come and go through the office it will be much easier to keep track of everything. Let's have a look at the other hut over there away from the others. I noticed as we parked the van that it has large doors like a garage and that they were shut tight.'

They moved across the site, lighting their way with only occasional flashes of torchlight. The moon was playing hide and seek among the light fleecy clouds, alternately illuminating the scene with a bright white light and then diving behind a cloud to give a dimmer more diffused glow which made seeing for any distance difficult.

They had occasionally to make their way round the huge stationary shapes of parked earthmoving machinery. Far too big and unwieldy to be put away at night in the sheds which housed the smaller tractors, they seemed to squat where their drivers had left them, looking like long forgotten dinosaurs in the uncertain moonlight. Cooling metal in the powerful engines cracked loudly in the stillness, proving that not very long ago these monsters had been working, levelling and filling the valley bottom.

The heavy, rich smell of hot oil and diesel fuel filled the air, making Marion's nose sting and her eyes water a little. David was breathing in the powerful fumes with an unconscious pleasure. This was a scent which any boy of his generation could only revel in.

Suddenly his nose wrinkled in disgust. The gentle breeze which was blowing through the saddle-like gap at the opposite end of the valley was carrying with it an alien smell which David could not identify. It was an unpleasant smell with a chemical ingredient that rang a warning bell in David's mind. It seemed to be getting stronger as they approached the sharp edge of the man-made platform, and the shed that was their immediate destination.

This building was different from the others. It was much larger and of a stronger construction. The sides were lined with steel sheets and the doors, made of the same sheet steel, were padlocked in two places with the same type of brass locks that had been used upon the office. The strange smell seemed to be coming from the building. High up in the wall was a small window. A large digger was parked by the side of the shed and Marion swung up onto the yellow bonnet to peer in through the window. 'It seems to be half full of oildrums,' she called down quietly. 'I think this is what we saw coming in on those lorries the other night. The shapes seem about right if you imagine them under a tarpaulin.' Marion climbed down and stood, dusting off her jeans with hands which were very little cleaner.

David turned to her as the moon made one of its periodic dashes between clouds and disappeared.

'I don't know what that smell is. I've never smelled it before, but it makes me think of death and decay.'

'Yes,' replied Marion. 'I know what you mean. I don't know much about building work, but I am fairly sure that it shouldn't smell like this.'

The two moved off to the edge of the man-made cliff and shone the torch down the steep loosely packed slope to the natural valley bottom below. The large pipe which carried the water from the stream underground below the building site extended for several yards beyond the rubble and loose soil, and the water running back into the stream bed looked thick and brackish.

As Marion let the torch play over the oily surface of the water, a movement caught the corner of her eye. She switched off the torch immediately and then put her hand gently on David's shoulder to catch his attention.

'Look out there,' she whispered softly. 'Just away from the water's edge. Isn't that a badger?'

David looked where she was pointing and as his eyes grew accustomed to the relative darkness, he could see what appeared to be a male badger shuffling slowly away from the water's edge.

'He must have a sett somewhere on the hillside,' he said. 'But whatever is the matter with him? He is having trouble walking and he's weaving all over the place. I think he must be ill. Let me have the torch a moment.'

The powerful beam from the torch showed that there was indeed something wrong with the badger. His fur had fallen away in great patches, leaving angry looking sores on his skin. When he turned his head towards the light they could see that his eyes were half closed, mattered and running. David turned the torch away from the sick animal, a hard cold lump settling in his stomach, and shone the beam across the partially destroyed valley.

By the time this inspection was over both he and Marion were very angry indeed. There were several rabbits, a large grey coated mountain hare and a fox scattered along the stream banks. All were dead and all showed the same signs of suffering as the badger.

'They have been poisoned by something I think,' David said angrily. 'But I can't think why. Even if the developers wanted to get rid of them they wouldn't need to go to these lengths. As they filled up the valley the animals would have left anyway. They are destroying their homes and habitat. They had no need to destroy them as well.'

Marion had taken the torch from David's knee and was playing it up and down the steep bank of rubble, deliberately avoiding the places where the sad, bedraggled corpses of the animals lay.

As David talked on, venting his anger and frustration in a low voiced bitter attack on the unknown killers, she drew her own conclusions from the evidence before them.

'I don't think it happened like that,' she interrupted David's stream of invective. 'I think the animals were poisoned accidently. Look down there at the foot of the slope.' She indicated an area of loose dirt and rock with the torch beam. 'Do you see that grey sludge which is oozing out from between those two large boulders? I think that is what is killing the animals and I think that whatever it is, is in those drums we saw in the locked store shed.

They are being buried with the rubble and I'll bet that they are being dumped here unlawfully.'

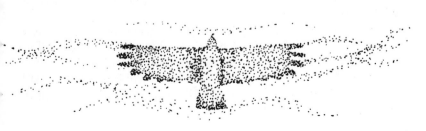

Outside the Factory Gates

The next day dawned bright and sunny, but Marion and David could not enjoy their perfect holiday surroundings. Since their discoveries of the previous evening high up on the moor in the ruined, hidden valley, their investigations had taken on a different, much more intense sense of purpose.

They had known from the start that Herne, the ancient, elemental spirit who was their mentor and guide, had been deeply disturbed by the work which was going on in the valley. Until, however, they had discovered the plight of the animals who had lived there for generations, they had not been able to understand his concern and anger.

Now they were both feeling this anger for themselves, and were determined to do anything they could to halt the steady creep of the deadly infill of industrial waste, for this is what they had decided must be in the buried drums, down the length of the natural valley floor.

'I suppose we could report what we have found to the Health Department at the Town Hall,' said David, as they sat over a cup of coffee in the hotel lounge. 'But we still don't know where the poison is coming from, or what the link with the developers is. It is possible that Mr Roper has no idea what is going on at all.'

'I can't believe that he can,' replied Marion. 'That holiday village is a very expensive project and to endanger it all for a little extra illegal profit just doesn't seem to make sense. I agree with you though. We don't have enough evidence yet to report it all to the authorities. Let's follow it through ourselves a little more.'

David smiled fondly at her.

'I was hoping you would say that,' he grinned. 'I have been thinking and it occurs to me that we can find out where the drums are coming from quite easily. That store shed was only half full when you looked in last night, which means it will not be long before another delivery is sent in. If we watch the road through the village we will know when they are delivering and we can follow one of the trucks when it leaves. That should lead us to wherever the drums are originating from.'

They had spent several pleasant evenings in the company of the local inhabitants of the village inn before the tinkling sound of vibrating glasses on the shelves behind the bar heralded the rumbling passage of several heavy lorries through the main street of the tiny village, outside the windows of the King's Head. Marion reached across the back of the low window seat and pulled aside the curtain.

'I'm sure they are the same trucks,' she whispered quietly, 'and they are heading in the direction of the valley. The same route that Sid, the farmer, took when he left here that first night.'

'Good!' nodded David. 'Now all we have to do is wait for them coming back. I have been dreading Sid coming in here for a drink each night we have been here. I'm glad we can get on with something at last.'

The young couple sat as long as they dared in the King's Head but just before the landlord began to gather up the glasses and make obvious preparations for closing for the night, they took their leave of him and the other customers. Settling down in the van in a small lane end on the edge of the village, they continued their watch for the empty, returning trucks.

It was not to be a long wait. The first lorry swept past their hiding place just as the digital clock on the dashboard of the van clicked over to show eleven thirty, and the lights of two more showed themselves at the same time winding down off the moor. As these two passed, David slipped the van into gear and pulled out into the road behind them.

'I'm not sure how many passed through the village on the way up,' he mused, 'but if we follow these two at a reasonable distance, we should be able to see if any more are coming up behind. They will have no idea that we are suspicious of what they are doing.'

The lorries set a fast pace and were soon entering the outskirts of Stockport. David tried to stay a little way back from his quarry, wherever possible, keeping a car or two between himself and the back truck. As they passed the shopping centre, dark and shuttered for the night, a police car pulled out into the steady trickle of traffic between the van and the vehicles it was following.

'If only they knew!' groaned Marion.

'Never mind,' laughed David. 'As soon as we have a little more information, we can tell the police and everyone else what is going on up there.'

The police car continued on its innocent way, and soon turned off into what appeared to be a small, modern industrial estate.

The traffic was thinning now and it was becoming harder for David to remain inconspicuous as he trailed the lorries. They had turned off the main road and were now deep into the straggle of factories, warehouses and run down, neglected shops and houses, which seem to surround the smart new centre of every city in the world.

Manchester was no exception and after just a few turns the young detectives had no idea where they were in relation to any of the main roads through the city centre. They were just beginning to realize that they were thoroughly lost when another problem presented itself. The leading waggon suddenly turned off the road they were following whilst the following one continued straight on.

'Now what do we do?' cried Marion in an agony of indecision. 'This was something we didn't count on.'

'I'm not sure what they are up to,' answered David. 'But I don't think it matters too much. As long as we keep following one of them, it should lead us eventually to where they came from'

David was proved right in the next few minutes. The lorry they had been following for so long began to slow down after a tortuous series of twists and turns through ever narrowing side streets, and eventually stopped outside a huge pair of steel gates. The driver sounded his horn in two short blasts and the gates swung apart and inwards to allow the waggon to pass.

David had stopped the van some way back from the gates, and now eased it forward again to where he could see a dark opening between two tall buildings on the opposite side of the road. He passed the narrow alleyway and then, switching off all the lights, reversed the van until the bonnet was far enough back in the shadows between the towering buildings to be invisible from the road. He sat back in his chair with a sigh, easing his position by lifting himself up on his hands and rocking gently forwards and back.

'Are you all right?' asked Marion, a worried note creeping into her voice. She was just beginning to realize that David had been at the wheel of the van for a long time without a break, and she had no way of knowing how his disability would affect him.

'I'm fine. Just a little stiff from being in one position for a long time. Don't worry about me.' David spoke in a light, teasing tone but he was secretly very pleased to find this pretty, intelligent girl was worried about him.

'Why have you hidden the van again?' asked Marion. 'Can't we just read what it says on that notice board by the gate and go home?'

'I'm waiting for the other truck,' replied David. 'If I'm right in my guess, they were both coming here, but split up and took a different way for the last part of the journey, so as not to draw too much attention to the fact that a lot of lorries come and go from here during the night. . . . Ah ha! I was right! Here comes the other one.'

A lorry was indeed nosing slowly out from another alley further up the road and as it drew nearer both of the young people in the van could see that it was the same one they had been following from the moorland village. It followed the same procedure as the previous truck, halting and signalling with two short blasts of its horn before swinging in through the gates.

'It should be safe now, I think,' said David. 'Can you read the board as you walk past? I don't think it would be a good idea to stand and stare at it at this time of night. We have no

115

way of knowing who might be watching.'

'I'll do my best,' called back Marion, as she slipped out of the van and walked rapidly away from the gates keeping in the shadows.

After she had gone a hundred metres down the road she stepped out into the relatively bright light of a street lamp and crossed the road, sauntering back along the high fence which led to the now tightly shut gates. She tried hard to give the impression of a late night reveller or perhaps a shift worker going gratefully home to bed.

The notice board was attached at eye level to the fence and it proved an easy task to read what the faded letters said as she strolled past, and then continue on her way to the next corner in the road. Once she had rounded the bend and was out of sight of the factory gates, she recrossed the road and, hugging the shadows once more, made her way back towards where David was anxiously waiting.

Marion was almost at the van and beginning to relax when the noise of an idling engine and a fuzzy, defused light, shining on the wall of the factory behind her, told her that a vehicle was approaching slowly down the street. She froze for an instant, her head swinging from side to side, seeking a place to hide. She felt very exposed now as the shadows she had relied upon to hide her, began to break up.

Her frantic searching revealed a large rubbish skip standing half on the road and half on the narrow pavement, straddling the kerb and surrounded by assorted rubbish from the various factories in the street. Marion sighed with relief as she squeezed between the wall and the skip as the lorry finally rounded the bend in the road and illuminated the pavement she had been walking on just a split second before.

Once again the gates opened and swallowed up the empty truck. Marion wriggled out of her hiding place and ran for the alley where the van was parked.

'I thought you might have been seen when the lorry came round the corner,' said David, his obvious concern for her safety making his voice shake a little. 'Did you find out anything?'

'I just managed to get out of sight, thank goodness.' Marion's voice was also a little shakey as she recounted her

116

narrow escape. She had not forgotten the rough way that the men had acted at the valley building site, when Sid had trapped them with his tractor, and she had no wish to repeat the experience in a back street of the city.

'The factory is owned by a firm called Industrial Chemical Factors Ltd. which would seem to agree with our theory, but the interesting thing is that under the main name it says in smaller print, A MEMBER OF THE ROPER GROUP OF COMPANIES.'

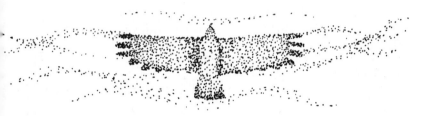

A Helpful Friend

The sun was quite high in the sky before David and Marion had the chance to discuss the night's discoveries. Marion had returned to her tent to sleep as the dawn light spread over the countryside, and David had spent what little remained of the night on the narrow bunk in the van. It had hardly seemed worth returning to the hotel and running the risk of disturbing the other guests. Both young people had slept more soundly and for far longer than they had intended. The activities of the night before had left them tired and drained as their excitement had steadied throughout their return to the Peaks.

The hot sun had finally made the air inside Marion's small tent uncomfortable and she had woken slowly, dozing for a while, whilst she enjoyed the steamy heat and the strong smell of hot canvas and the crushed grass below the groundsheet.

The events of the night before came back to her as sleep receded and consciousness returned. She dressed and crawled out into the sunlight.

'Like a butterfly from its chrysalis,' she thought with a grin as she stretched her arms above her head and, bending swiftly, touched her toes. After a few moments of vigorous exercise she crossed to the parked van and banged on the side.

'Are you going to sleep all day in there?' she called, and a sleepy voice replied,

'I was intending to, yes. But as I'm awake now I might as well get up. I'll be with you in a minute, put the kettle on for a coffee. We need to talk.'

David spoke slowly and hesitantly, trying to voice thoughts which were not really completely formed.

'It seems obvious to me, whatever is in those drums which Roper's men are burying in the valley, is a toxic waste of some sort which is poisoning the animals. I have no doubt that Roper is quite sure that it is safe because it's in sealed containers, but we know that at least one has burst and is leaking.' Marion nodded.

'Yes,' she whispered, the horror of seeing the suffering badger still very fresh in her mind. 'But what is it, and why isn't it being dumped on an official site where it can be disposed of under proper supervision?'

David was quiet for several seconds as he gathered his thoughts. Then he spoke with growing conviction.

'What if that chemical factory is making a harmless, everyday product which is sold in the normal way as a front to hide the fact that it is also manufacturing something else? Something which is illegal and very dangerous. Maybe a poison gas, or some type of chemical weapon for sale abroad to small countries. There are lots of them who are always at war with their neighbours. It could even be sold to revolutionaries, or terrorists. If that was the case they would have to dispose of any waste product secretly or it would be traced back to them, and the government would find out what they were doing.'

'That all sounds very likely to me,' grinned Marion. 'But how are we going to find out if your theory is anywhere near the right one, and if it is, how can we find proof?'

'I think I may know where to start,' replied David. 'I need to go back to the hotel to shower and change. While I'm there I can use the phone. I have a friend from university who can help us, and the hotel phone is very convenient. I have trouble fitting my chair into a phone box. Why don't you start making us some breakfast, or is it lunch, and I'll be back soon?'

David arrived back at the camp site just as Marion was putting the finishing touches to the small camp table she had laid on the grass outside her tent. She continued to fill two plates with thick rashers of sizzling bacon and fat, brown country sausages from the pan on the calor gas stove, as David launched excitedly into reiterating what his friend had

119

said.

'Please, David,' laughed Marion, as she topped off their meal with a couple of dark yellow yoked eggs from the farm across the field. 'Start again, from the beginning this time. Who is this friend of yours, and how can he help us?'

'Sorry!' grinned David ruefully. 'Bill was studying for a science degree at the university and graduated at the same time as I did. He has got a job with the Public Health Department of his local council and I wondered if he might have any ideas about our problem. I described the badger to him and told him about the dead animals and birds in the valley and about the dreadful smell. He thinks the sludge may well be a dioxin, a poison which is used in the manufacture of certain weedkillers. Quite a lot of them are illegal here, but are still used in some other countries, particularly some of the South American ones.

He wants us to try and get a sample of the sludge from the site, so that he can test it and find out if it really is what he thinks.'

'We should have thought of that ourselves,' groaned Marion, in exasperation. 'We should have known we would need a sample, but we were so upset and angry at what we had seen, that neither of us was thinking very straight, were we? I suppose we will have to go back to the valley again tonight if the men and trucks are not there.'

David gave a sigh of relief. He had been trying to think of a way of suggesting just this course of action for some time, but, knowing Marion's feelings and apprehensions about their last visit to the site, he had been reluctant to ask her to go through it all again.

David spent the rest of the day working at the desk in the back of his vehicle. He made a series of rough notes which covered all the important points of their investigation to date, and then pulled out from its locker below the tiny desk his portable battery powered computer. Switching it to its word processing mode he began to expand his rough, handwritten notes into a full and comprehensive report.

Marion looked on admiringly, occasionally correcting a word or a phrase as they appeared on the small screen if she felt that they would give a wrong impression to the reader, or if she could think of a better way to express their feelings.

Both the young people were quietly surprised and delighted at the way in which they found they could work together. David had spent countless solitary hours with his computer and sheaves of wildlife notes but he had always felt that he could not allow anyone, not even his parents or his sister Sara, to read what he had written until the finished article was polished to his satisfaction. Now he realized that he was enjoying wholeheartedly the feeling that another person could help him in his work.

Marion, for her part, was discovering a talent which, until now, she did not know she possessed. She found that to be able to help David in his work at the computer was very satisfying and the feeling that they were blending their knowledge and skills to become a competent, working team was very, very good.

Neither of them made any comment on the fact that the report made no mention of Herne the Hunter, or about his part in their adventure. They both felt that their involvement with the ancient god was too private and personal to be included and that nobody in the industrial, modern world would believe that he existed.

David put the finishing touches to the manuscript as the light was failing and the afterglow from the dark red, sinking sun, long since vanished behind the hills was slanting into the van from an impossibly low angle. He sat back with a sigh, pressing the keys to transfer the report to a small floppy disk in the drive below the keyboard and reached into the cupboard over his head for an envelope. He addressed the long brown envelope to the office of his publisher in London and when the computer had finished rattling and chuckling to itself he placed the disk inside, sealed it up and stamped it. Marion was looking at him with a puzzled expression.

'Why the hurry?' she asked. 'We should be able to finish the story one way or the other in a few days.'

David was looking serious, and not a little worried.

'I will feel a lot happier going down into that valley tonight if the information we have gathered so far is on its way to London. Now, how about supper at the King's Head before we head up on to the moor?'

Prisoners

The steep rutted track once again made the van twist and
shake uncomfortably as it crept down towards the dark,
deserted building site. No lights showed in the windows of
the buildings or the cabs of the huge earthmoving machinery. Only the several yards of new, level gravel, which
extended beyond the last building, bore witness to the work
which had been going on in the intervening time since the
two young investigators had made their last secretive visit to
the valley.

They had eaten a good hearty meal in the small lounge of
the King's Head in the village below the moor, chatting to the
landlord and some of the local people, whilst always keeping
an ear open for the sound of the trucks from the chemical
works rumbling through the tiny village street.

The pub had closed at a little after eleven o'clock. David
and Marion had judged the time right to climb up onto the
high moor to continue their investigation of the hidden
valley.

David pulled the van between the last two buildings in the
row, an open sided garage containing a tractor, and the
large, securely padlocked store where they were sure that
the drums of toxic waste were stacked ready for burying with
the soil and gravel, with which the valley was being levelled.
Marion slipped down from the cab to the gravel plain and
looked cautiously around.

'It seems to be all right,' she called back to David. 'Come
on.' The small electric motor on the rear hoist of the van
hummed for a moment, and David wheeled his chair
towards the edge of the artificial plateau.

'I'm afraid you will have to climb down to the valley floor,' he said. 'I'm not very good on steep slopes.'

Marion nodded, smiling to herself at David's humour. She took the torch from his lap and shone it down the face of the huge scree slope to the valley floor. Several birds lay dead on the grass at the foot of the slope and the water which trickled out of the pipe protruding from the rubble of the slope was oily looking and brackish.

She shuddered as she thought of the animals and birds which must already be buried under all those tons of earth and stone, and the harm which could be brought to the village below if the poison which ran through the valley was to get into their water supply. She knew that the water from these hills seeped down through fissures in the rock into the potholes and caves below, and after sinking to incredible depths was forced up into the natural springs for which the Peak District was famous. The aftermath of this greedy business man's irresponsible and criminal actions could be felt twenty years into the future of this peaceful, rural area.

David's friend, Bill, the scientist, had explained some of the long term effects of the toxic dioxin waste. Both the domestic animals on the farms in the lower lands below and the wild life which drank from the springs and streams which had been contaminated, would suffer painful stomach cramps, difficulty in breathing and run the risk of producing malformed or stillborn young.

'It could be years,' she thought, 'before someone thinks to trace the source of the poison to this valley in the hills, and by that time Mr Roper and his corrupt business empire will be gone. He will be living abroad and be able to deny all knowledge of the terrible suffering he will have caused.'

Marion shook herself firmly. This was not the time to dwell on what might be. It was in her's and David's power to stop this cruel man and she must concentrate on doing exactly that. She handed the heavy torch back to David.

'Try and keep the beam just ahead of me,' she instructed him. 'I have a small flashlight of my own in my pocket which I can use when I get to the bottom.'

David rolled the chair to the edge and locked the brakes firmly. He watched apprehensively as Marion began her descent but he soon realized that her nimble figure was flitting lightly down the loose scree, picking out the larger, more deeply imbedded boulders on which to place her feet, and that she was in no danger as long as he could keep the beam of the torch positioned to illuminate her way.

Soon Marion reached the bottom of the slope and turned to wave reassuringly up at him before setting off along the lower edge to explore. He watched as the tiny beam from her pocket torch danced among the rocks and rubble as she searched for the tell-tale grey sludge seeping from the loose earth. After a few moments the light disappeared.

David started up in his chair in alarm, a feeling of intense frustration at being stuck so far above where Marion may be in danger flooding his mind, before reason once again took hold, as he realized that Marion had simply turned a corner around a particularly large boulder and that her flashlight was now visible again probing the shadows.

It seemed a long time to David until the slim figure of the girl stood below him again. Even from his elevated position on the top of the slope he could sense her disappointment. It was apparent in the droop of her shoulders and her slow step as she began her climb back up to the level top of the infill. It came as no surprise when she called up from where she was resting for a moment on a round topped boulder of limestone.

'I can't find any of the poison. The workmen have long since buried the part of the valley floor we saw before, and it seems that none of the drums they have buried more recently have leaked. I have picked up several of the dead birds. Perhaps Bill can trace the poison in their bodies, but then, how can we prove that it came from here?'

David opened his mouth to call down a reassuring reply to the disappointed girl, when suddenly he froze. The building site all around him was transformed from a shadowy, half hidden place to a stark white brilliance as huge floodlights snapped on. Marion flattened herself into the shadows of the rock as harsh white lights seemed to wash over the rim above her and the reflected brilliance turned the face of the slope into a patchwork of light and dark.

David spun his chair to face the buildings. He found he was looking at several men, spread out in a loose, undisciplined line between himself and the sheds, separating him from any hope of escape to the van. The line of men began to move threateningly towards him. David noticed that the two men in the middle were Sid, the farmer, and the man who had driven the jeep on the first occasion they had met at the top of the lane on the hill.

'So!' sneered Sid, as he swaggered across the intervening space. 'You couldn't keep away after all. I did warn you that snooping around here would be dangerous. Where is your girlfriend then? I'm sure you didn't come here on your own.'

David swallowed nervously, trying desperately to get his voice under strict control before he spoke. He was sure that letting Sid and the others know just how much their sudden appearance had startled him would not be a good idea.

'Marion didn't come with me tonight,' he said loudly, hoping that his voice would carry to where he was sure Marion was crouching on the face of the slope behind him. 'She was too frightened of what would happen if we were caught. She is waiting for me back at her camp site. . . I suppose she will be worried if I don't turn up there again soon,' he added as an afterthought. Sid did not seem very impressed with David's attempt to rattle him.

'Never mind that now,' he grated. 'It's hours until morning yet, and she won't begin to worry until it gets light at least.' He turned to the other men who were grouped round David's chair and ordered gruffly, 'Bring him along to the office. We can lock him up there until we decide what to do with him.'

He was bundled into the room at the back of the office, the men picking up his chair and roughly hurling it, and him in it, up the steps and through the larger room. He came to rest, rocking precariously, against the bags of cement piled near the back wall.

David gasped as he brought his laboured breathing under control. He seemed to be in one piece, he thought, just a little bruised from the rough handling of his chair. At least Marion was still free. He was sure that she would prove resourceful enough to escape from the valley and get help.

'Every cloud has a silver lining,' he thought, feeling more cheerful with every passing minute. 'What more proof do we need that something very wrong is going on? The police will find me locked up in here when Marion brings them to the rescue, and they will have to listen and believe us then.'

The door crashed open against the stacks of small tools which were stored behind it, dispelling his confident musings like so much smoke in a mountain breeze. David hardly had time to turn his chair towards the disturbance, before a kicking, scratching ball of fighting energy was propelled through the opening. The door slammed shut.

'Hello,' gasped Marion, when she had recovered her breath a little. 'I made it to the van and was going to hide inside until it quietened down, and then try to escape. But I couldn't leave without finding out if you were all right. So I sneaked over here to see if I could see you. . . . I didn't see the guard in the shadows by the door until he grabbed me,' she finished lamely. 'Sorry, David. What are we going to do now?'

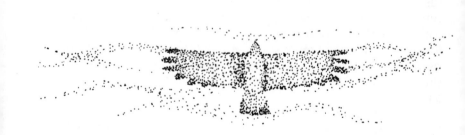

Saved!

They had tried to sleep until dawn brought a heavy shower of rain which beat on the roof of the wooden office building. It echoed hollowly, waking up the two fitfully sleeping occupants of the locked room at the rear, with a start.

When both of them were fully awake Marion asked her question again. 'What are we going to do? We've been locked up in here all night, and we're no nearer to escaping now than we were before.'

David tried hard to sound optimistic as he replied. 'Things could be a lot worse,' he said. 'When my publisher gets that disk with our story on it, he will ring the hotel. When they tell him they don't know where I am and that I haven't been back for a day or so he will begin to worry. The disk gives the location of the valley very clearly and it won't be long before he alerts the police. I hope,' he added silently, not feeling quite so confident as he had tried to sound for Marion's sake.

They sat in silence for an hour or more, trying to hear what the two men in the outer office were saying, but apart from an odd name and a very mumbled conversation which appeared to be on the telephone, they could glean nothing of much use. David raised his head suddenly and turned towards the door in the outside wall of the room.

'Did you hear that?' he said. 'It sounded like a car coming down the track. Perhaps we will find out what they intend to do with us now.'

'I think I can answer that, David,' whispered Marion softly. 'But I don't think you will like it one bit. That car sounded very like mine to me, and I do know the sound of its engine very well.

'I think they must have sent someone to fetch it from the camp site last night. I have no doubt that they will have packed up my tent and things as well. All the farmer will see is the empty space when he walks round this morning to collect his fee, and as I paid every morning for the day he will think I packed up and left early.'

David blanched.

'If they are going to this much trouble to hide our whereabouts, then they must intend getting rid of us for good,' he said bitterly. 'Nothing else makes sense after the way they have treated us. I suppose they intend us to become part of the infill in this valley. We must think of a way out.'

The day wore on slowly and tediously. David and Marion became very hungry and thirsty as nobody came near their prison to feed them or give them water. The steady rumble of the heavy earthmoving machinery began a little after eight o'clock and continued until midday when they heard bursts of laughter from the office. Marion decided that the small core of workmen who must know what was going on were gathered there to eat their lunch. After a short break the machinery started up again and the office became quiet.

It was almost six o'clock when the inner door swung open and they were confronted by the architect, Mr Warwick, wringing his hands and shaking uncontrollably. He was talking rapidly as he came through the door.

'Why didn't you listen to me when I told you to keep away from here?' he said almost pleadingly. 'I knew you would get yourselves into trouble, and I was right. I don't know what we're going to do with you now. This operation is much too important for you to be allowed to upset it. You see if anyone finds out about this, then Mr Roper's whole empire will come tumbling down. He has done all sorts of things which won't bear too much looking at.' Warwick paused for breath, and David took the opportunity to ask a question of his own.

'Why have you had Marion's car brought here?' he asked sharply, 'and how did you know where to go?' Warwick flinched visibly.

'We have been watching you ever since you asked about the plans at the Council offices,' he wheezed, choosing not to answer the first part of David's question. Turning on his heel, he left the room, looking very flustered.

Shortly after that they heard a car drive away from the office and begin the long climb out of the valley.

'That will be Warwick leaving us to our fate,' David said. 'But unless my ears deceive me, he may have given us a way out of here.' He lowered his voice until Marion had to strain to hear him. 'I don't think he remembered to lock the door, he was so agitated.'

'If only the men in the office don't notice and leave us alone until it's gone a bit darker, we may have a chance,' grinned Marion. 'We must think of a way to distract them when the time is right. We will need to get you down the steps in your chair and over to the van without being seen, and that is a very tall order indeed.'

'I have a plan,' whispered back David, 'which may make that a bit easier. If you can get to the van and reverse it over to the office door, then the hoist should drop down onto the top step and I can shoot almost straight in to the driving position. It will save a lot of time and effort and make our escape much easier. First I need to tell you how to drive the van and operate the hoist. The hand controls will seem awkward to you. You won't want to be fumbling with them in the heat of the moment.'

Time passed until the two youngsters judged that it would be dark enough outside the hut to aid their escape. Still, however, they had not thought of a way to distract their two guards. They could still hear a faint mumbling of conversation through the door, which told them that just to burst out into the office would be foolish.

They were beginning to despair when a dog began to bark quite near to the hut, and a scratching noise began under the front of the building. No sooner had these sounds faded into an intense quiet, than the bellowing of several cows rent the air at the back of the hut and the thud of heavy horns hitting the outside door could be heard.

A cry of surprise rang out from the office, followed by a string of bad language. The office door crashed open. They could hear the men shouting in confusion outside.

'Get out of here.'

'Where did they come from?'

'They must have wandered down off the moor.'

Marion crept to the door of the office and risked opening it a crack to look through. She was in time to see one of the guards running down the steps brandishing a pickaxe handle over his head, to drive the herd of cows away.

As he reached the bottom step a small black and white shape streaked from under the hut and fastened its teeth into his leg with an audible crunch. The man screamed in surprise and pain. He fell, rolling headlong across the gravel, trying in vain to shake loose the grip of the old badger, which was attached firmly to his leg. After rolling for several yards he managed to regain his feet and to shake loose the maddened animal. He turned to look for the club he had dropped when he had fallen, but was faced with not one snarling, growling badger, but a whole family of them, all very angry and all intent, it seemed, on harming him.

He backed away slowly, across the flat plain, aware that he was heading for the man-made cliff but not able to do anything about it. As he approached the edge he turned, intending to run as fast as his injured leg would carry him, around the angry animals and back to the safety of the office.

It was a good plan, and should have worked, except that the limping man had not taken into account the lithe red fox which waited just out of sight under the rim of the cliff. As he turned to begin his run and lunged away from the badgers, the fox slipped between his legs.

The second guard emerged from the office in time to see his friend apparently hurl himself over the edge of the drop into the darkness below. He began to run. He skidded to a halt by the place where his mate had vanished, just as Marion burst from the office door. She made a mad dash for the alley between the two huts where the van was parked. As she ran, she chanted over and over in her head the instructions David had given her to get the vehicle in motion, and to operate the hoist when she had reversed to the steps.

The man on the cliff edge sensed her movement and began to swing back towards her. He did not have time to complete the turn. A huge bird hurled from the sky and struck him a crashing blow across the shoulders, catapulting him down the slope to lie with the unconscious guard at the

Escape

131

bottom, half in and half out of the stream where it trickled from the mouth of the pipe.

Herne, for Herne it was in his eagle form, swept up and away, crying to the animals of his kingdom to get away.

'The job is done. Well done! Well done!'

Marion collapsed panting against the door of the van, and began frantically unlocking the door. She had heard Herne's cries, and understood enough to know that they were safe for the moment. She had no way of knowing, however, whether the two men were even now clawing their way back up the loose scree of the slope, or how much time she had to rescue David and get away.

The locks clicked as the central locking system released all the doors, and Marion climbed swiftly in, kneeling in front of the steering wheel in the empty well where David's wheelchair would normally be clamped. The engine started on the first turn of the key and Marion dropped the gearstick into reverse, flipping on the switch which would illuminate the rear of the vehicle and the hoist when the doors were opened. The van shot backwards, out into the open. She crossed the space between the huts in a few seconds, and slowed to a crawl as she approached the office steps. David was waiting on the top step and flung open the rear doors before she had brought the van to a stop. He was almost level with the floor of the van and it was the work of a moment to reach the handset from the rack where it was kept and to lower the hoist on to the step. Marion climbed into the passenger seat, as David's chair thumped into the clamps on the floor and the van sped away from the steps.

Marion heaved a great sigh of relief. They were safe at last. David accelerated away across the building site but as he approached the two huts nearest to the entrance to the track, he braked hard, skidding the vehicle into the shadows between them. He stopped the engine and turned out all the lights.

'What are you doing now?' cried Marion 'Let's get going while we still can.' David pointed up the track.

'I'm fairly sure there is a vehicle of some sort coming through the cutting onto the track,' he replied. 'The rocks at the entrance seemed to stand out in some sort of light. I noticed it as I lined up the van for the run up. . . There!' he added. 'I thought so.' As he spoke a powerful pair of headlights pierced the darkness above them, shining out over the steep drop and turning in line with the first level of the track. They were closely followed by a second pair, brighter than the first but moving much more slowly.

David reached up to the overhead console and lifted down the microphone from the radio. After switching on the set and tuning it to the frequency he wanted, he began urgently to call. After a few seconds an official sounding voice echoed from the speaker above their heads.

'This is an official channel. Please retune your set immediately. I repeat, this is an official police channel.'

David grinned in relief and began to speak. He had no sooner replaced the handset of the radio and switched off when the lights of the vehicles on the track swept past their hiding place and swung to a halt on the gravel.

There was enough light from the moon to see that they were a rather battered pick-up truck, its open back full of very rough looking men, and looking very incongruous, a gold coloured Rolls Royce with a peak-capped driver. A large fat man almost filled the back seat.

David leaned across to Marion and whispered. 'I'll bet that is Mr Roper himself, and these are the men who have been dumping the drums of waste at night. They must have come to dump us tonight. Check your seat belt. This may get a little rough.'

The engine of the powerful van burst into life as David switched on all the lights and hurled the vehicle out on to the track. All four tyres slid and then bit into the rough surface as they began the long climb at a very dangerous speed. The van rocked madly from side to side.

Glancing out of the rear window, Marion shouted, 'They're after us, David.' The van swayed round the first bend. 'Do be careful.'

They climbed ever higher, sliding from side to side of the track, sometimes narrowly missing the rocky wall on one side and then swinging over to bounce perilously close to the edge of the drop. Whenever they were near the outer edge, David could see that the pick-up was slowly gaining on him but that the Rolls, which was a much heavier vehicle and not

133

made for this type of driving, was falling a long way behind. He realized that they were going to be caught before they reached the top of the track, but there seemed nothing else to do but keep on and to hope for the best.

A shadow suddenly flickered across the glass panel of the sunroof. The familiar shape of Herne, the eagle, flashed over the roof of the van and dived, claws extended towards the face of the driver of the pick-up.

There was a sheet of toughened glass windscreen between the terrified driver and those tearing talons, but his terror made the man forget that. This was a primaeval attacker and a primitive fear which made him wrench the wheel across to save himself.

The truck launched itself out over the drop and, spilling screaming men down the slope, turned slowly over in the air before landing with a rending crash on the track below, right in the path of the struggling Rolls Royce. The driver had no chance to avoid the wrecked pick-up and the front end of the immaculate car crunched into scrap with the impact.

David slowed down and took the van carefully through the rocky defile into the shallow valley beyond. He was immediately surrounded by shadowy figures shining torches and wearing dark blue uniforms. He braked to a stop and opened the window to speak to the tall police inspector who peered in.

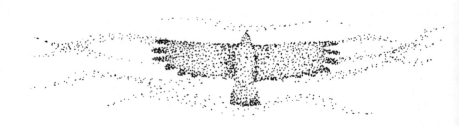

Champions Triumphant!

The previous two hours had been satisfying ones for David and Marion. They had watched Mr Roper and his men being brought up from the valley below, under arrest and looking very much the worse for their night's misadventures.

They had told their story to a succession of ever more important police officers, seated comfortably in the small lounge bar of the King's Head which had been commandeered for the occasion.

'It will make an excellent incident room,' the inspector who had been the first to arrive on the scene had said, grinning and casting a pleased eye over the pumps on the small bar.

Now, it seemed that all the excitement was over for the two young people. The local police were in touch with the force which had jurisdiction over the area of the city where Roper's factory was located. Both the Manchester and the London Police had been alerted. They would all be making early morning raids on the factory and offices of the Roper empire and they confidently expected to find records and other evidence which would break the evil businessman's power for ever.

'You two have done a wonderful job of work,' chuckled the inspector. 'It seems that the London fraud squad have had their eye on Roper for some time, but they couldn't find any evidence to start an investigation into his affairs. Now that you have uncovered what I think will be the tip of the iceberg, we can really get cracking.'

'What about Sid, the farmer from Underhill?' asked David. 'And Mr Warwick, the architect?'

'I wouldn't like to think of anything too drastic happening to Warwick,' added Marion. 'He never seemed to be a bad man, just very frightened all the time. I think he was drawn into Roper's activities just by being weak. Then when he realized how far they were prepared to go to keep us quiet, he deliberately left that door unlocked to give us a chance.'

David was nodding his head in emphatic agreement.

'I really don't care what happens to the gruesome Sid,' he laughed. 'But Marion is quite right about Warwick. I'm sure he tried to help us to escape.'

'It's not up to me of course,' the inspector smiled at their anxious expressions. 'I will, however, make a note of what you have said, and I am sure that any judge will take that into account. Sid is under arrest with the others in the station at Buxton and will be charged in the morning. He swears that he didn't know anything about the chemical dump and that he thought you were just trespassers, but I'm sure he will tell a different tale in the morning.

'Roper also swears that he knew nothing about what was going on. He is suggesting that Sid and some of the men were behind the dumping on the site. It won't take long for us to get the full story now the ring leaders are starting to fall out amongst themselves.'

'What really worries me,' said David softly, 'is what will happen to the hidden valley now? It will be no use for the holiday development and all those drums of poison are still buried there.'

'It's early days yet for decisions like that.' The inspector looked pensive. 'But, if everything you told us is proved to be true, then the authorities will have to dig up the drums to dispose of them on a safe site somewhere. The building development was planned by Roper and I doubt if his firm will withstand the publicity that his trial will bring, even if he manages to wriggle out of being sent to prison in some way.

'I suspect the valley will be more or less returned to its natural state and left to the wildlife for a good while at least.'

David gave a huge sigh of relief.

'Herne will be pleased with that and us,' he grinned and

136

Marion smiled back at him.

'Yes,' she replied. 'I think we have done our job quite well.'

The inspector was looking puzzled.

'Who is this Herne chap? You mentioned that he helped you to escape from the hut on the site. I think we ought to interview him. His evidence may be helpful.'

David and Marion stared in consternation at the inspector, and then both collapsed into helpless laughter. It was some time before either of them could gather enough breath to give the policeman an intelligible answer.

'I really don't think that will be possible, Inspector,' David choked. 'You see, he travels around a lot and was only passing through here on his way to "somewhen" else. He doesn't like to get involved with the authorities if he can help it.'

'I see!' nodded the policeman, completely ignoring what he took to be David's slip of the tongue, and wrote in his notes, 'Mr Herne? No fixed abode.'

'I really think we should get some rest now, David,' said Marion. 'We still have several days of our holiday left and I really would like to see a bit more of the Peak District before I have to go home.'

As they crossed the car park to where the van and Marion's rescued car stood waiting, they stopped involuntarily and looked up into the night sky. There, directly above them, starkly silhouetted by the moon's white light, hung the shape of a golden eagle. David raised an arm in salute and continued on his way muttering to Marion, 'No fixed abode indeed! The whole earth is his abode.'

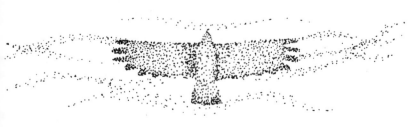